The Cowboy's Challenge

Donamae—
Thank you so much
for participating in
my giveaway— Happy
reading!

The Cowboy's Challenge

A Montana Rodeo Brides Romance

Sinclair Jayne

The Cowboy's Challenge

Tule Publishing First Printing, September 2021

The Tule Publishing, Inc.

First Publication by Tule Publishing 2021

Cover design by Lynn Andreozzi

ISBN: 978-1-954894-34-1

Chapter One

Grey's Saloon, Marietta, Montana. His favorite watering hole in America. And he'd been in a lot of them. But Grey's, with its worn, wide-planked floor that had survived the stomp of thousands of cowboy and cowgirl boots over its century and a half, and its wide, battered bar that had smoothed the slide of whiskeys straight up for the thirsty for just as long, was the best. And it was home. Or so he'd always believed.

Bowen Ballantyne turned away from his reflection in the tarnished and warped mirror behind the bar and stared moodily at the dance floor that was surprisingly busy for a Sunday night. Too early for most cowboys to be hitting town to prepare for the Copper Mountain Rodeo next weekend but eager to arrive at the ranch to see their granddad, Bowen and his two cousins had hopped in their rigs the minute their events at the Panhandle Rodeo had wrapped and driven home.

Home. Damn. That word again.

He'd ignored the two beers his cousin Bodhi had ordered for him and instead picked up his whiskey and stared at the amber liquid like it had the answers he needed. He was the oldest. He needed to figure out a solution to the problem Granddad had casually dumped in their laps tonight—he was thinking of selling the ranch. The idea was as out there as a one-hundred-point ride. Five generations of Ballantynes. For as long as he could remember, the three of them had planned to join Granddad at Three Tree Ranch. Sure, they knew they'd have to have side gigs—the ranch was massive, but not economically viable to support all of them initially. But that's why they'd busted it on the pro rodeo for the past handful of years, saved their money, invested.

He and his cousins—Bodhi and Beck—would need to sit down to see if they had enough to offer on the ranch. They'd never figured Granddad would sell. It had always been handed down. The money they'd saved had been to make improvements on the ranch, take care of Granddad's needs if and when he decided to retire—even that concept seemed foreign. Granddad epitomized hands-on.

So what was up?

Had his mom and two aunts put too much pressure on him? Had he finally caved?

And since all the moms were descending on Tuesday "to spruce up the ranch for sale, and give Papa one last Ballantyne Bash to remember," Bowen doubted their combined rodeo earnings and investments would begin to cut into the multimillion-dollar sale price his real estate mogul mother would dream up. Sure, all three of them were top earners on the pro tour and had their fair share of endorsements, but they weren't the pop stars, A-list actors or tech start-up kingpins his mom had in her client base. She'd even gushed about a new K-pop star client she had. Bowen hadn't even imagined his mom knew what K-pop was. Heck, he wasn't sure he did.

Without the ranch, Bowen would feel lost, and he was sure his granddad would too—his mom and aunts would see to that. Not deliberately. They just thought they knew better than any man alive.

Of course they were all long single. And pretty happy about it from all Bowen could tell. Not that he could point a finger. He'd never once had a serious relationship and didn't figure he'd change that stat anytime soon.

He held the whiskey to his lips but paused. The amber swirl caught the light and reminded him of a girl…what was her name? Little barrel racer in summer stock rodeo when he'd been a teen. She'd had eyes the color of whiskey and hair the color of clouds and a mouth that rarely stopped challenging him.

He shook his head.

Why was he thinking of her? Just because he was back in Marietta? What *was* her name? He remembered her nickname—the one he'd accidentally bestowed and Bodhi had used with reckless abandon. Damn, she'd been tough. Young. And obvious. And sweet. Too sweet. And another ranch kid who had to grow up tough because her daddy didn't stick around.

And as usual he'd been…aloof was the nicest way one woman had described him.

Bowen owned who and what he was.

"Dang, but that girl's drunk," his middle cousin Bodhi briefly interrupted his flirt session with an auburn-haired beauty to point out. "I think she's going to drown Beck. Time to launch a rescue?"

"Nope." Bowen looked away. The fact that Beck had been alone and pounced on by a determined, and quite drunk female was his own fault. He'd lost his focus this year—both on the rodeo and with his long-time girlfriend—and it looked like she might have either pulled the plug on his vacillating or she was making a point. No matter. Beck had been alone at Grey's and fair game, and he had no idea of the skill level of female hunters since he'd had Ashni by his side since high school.

"That's cold." Bodhi laughed, clearly enjoying schooling the beautiful woman he'd picked up on the art of shooting whiskey too much to interrupt his fun by bailing out his flailing cousin.

And Bowen was in no mood after his granddad's news. Hearing that his mom and both aunts were coming for the week had only made everything worse, and now Bodhi was proposing a Rodeo Bride Game.

Typical Bodhi.

Wildly creative and ridiculous with more than an outside chance of paying out.

Bodhi had barely let them order their first drink before he'd concocted the scheme: get engaged by the end of the Copper Mountain Rodeo and bring a prospective bride home to the Ballantyne Bash. Bodhi's rationale was that granddad would see that his grandsons were ready to settle down. He would have family around him at the ranch and feel the Ballantyne legacy at Three Trees Ranch was assured. He'd feel less pressure to sell. Then Beck had had to put in his two cents' worth. Now the engagement had to be public and showy, with Granddad and the moms becoming unwitting judges.

As if all three of them hadn't been judged and pitted against each other and everyone else since they'd exited the maternal Ballantyne wombs. And with Bowen being the oldest, he had to be the best. And watch out for the others—guide them, teach them, keep them safe.

Bodhi had made that job a bitch this season. He'd been reckless. Bold. Taking too many chances and not pacing himself. Burning it at both ends, as Granddad used to say.

And then because he'd had to put his boot in his mouth and make the whole…whatever Bodhi had created—a dare, a challenge, an alcohol-tinged impulse—into a game because he'd asked about a prize. He'd thought that would shut the whole thing down. It wasn't as if one of them could win the ranch. They all planned to settle there with Granddad. But no. Instead, he'd lit the funeral pyre.

Beck had shouted out Plum Hill.

The most beautiful, scenic, memory-evoking spot on the entire ranch—for all of them.

Bodhi had shut that down fast, but the fake engagement challenge was out there, and Bowen felt he had no recourse but to throw his hat into the ring. No matter how small or silly or crazy the slapped-down dare, challenge or competition was, Bowen didn't back down, and he always played to win.

Bodhi could probably persuade a woman to do almost anything, but the only thing Bodhi stuck was eight seconds on a bull or a saddleless bronc. Or saddle bronc when he was looking to twig Beck, as that was his specialty along with bulldogging.

Bowen was unconvinced that if he or Bodhi brought home a woman, swearing they'd fallen heads over boots with at the rodeo, their granddad would believe them. And Beck just had to drop to one knee in front of Ashni and pull out a sparkly and he'd have the deal cinched.

But why should Beck have everything handed to him?

He watched his cousin try to disentangle himself from the drunk bridesmaid once again. It was kinda sweet how Beck was trying his best to keep his hands in G-rated places while the woman kept aiming for the X-rated zone below Beck's new shiny buckle.

Arrogant show-off. Bowen had saved all his buckles but didn't rotate them for show. He still wore his first win as All-Around Cowboy at Copper Mountain Rodeo from twelve years ago. Marietta was home.

But would it still be if Granddad sold?

Did Bodhi's crazy scheme have a chance to work?

But if they didn't try to persuade Granddad to stay, the future would feel so uncertain. Bowen had never once considered settling anywhere but Marietta and the ranch. And he'd never be able to sit up on the massive granite rock in the old orchard and play his guitar and watch the stars come out. He'd never once envisioned his future without Three Tree Ranch and his granddad and cousins by his side.

He'd need to get Granddad alone. Talk to him. Man to man. If Granddad was being pressured, well, Bowen was a master at dodging the moms. If Granddad was short of money, all of them would help. If Granddad was ill—his stomach pitched—he could peel off the tour and take care of him. But that would leave Bodhi without an anchor. And Beck cut adrift without Ashni, possibly. Though Bowen didn't do long-term, he knew what an unhappy woman looked like. Ashni's light had dimmed this year.

"You're the oldest—help Beck out. He's too good for his own good," Bodhi mocked, interrupting Bowen's brooding.

The responsibility he wore as naturally as his Kevlar vest and chaps felt especially heavy tonight.

And for a moment, he kicked against it.

Beck was a big boy. He could launch his own extrication.

But that seemed less likely as the woman, grinding against him, wrapped her arms around him and started staggering toward the door. Too much liquor and high heels hampered a graceful exit.

To his credit, Beck tried to keep her upright and clearly had it in mind to somehow get the bridesmaid safely back to her table or home. Beck cast him an anxious glance, and Bowen felt the familiar tug of family war with his deep-set reticence and self-preservation to engage with drunk females. It never went well.

But family was family. And he'd had Beck's back since his mom had forced him to sit in a hard, white hospital chair, his legs dangling, and wrapped his toddler arms around the red-faced, screaming, blue-wrapped newborn.

"You're the oldest cousin. You look after Bodhi and now you look after Beckett. That's what Ballantynes do."

And he had.

Cowboy up.

He pushed away from the bar just as the drunk bridesmaid opened the swinging double doors with her hip and dragged Beck out into the night. As if his earlier thought of Ashni manifested her, Bowen saw Ashni and another woman with long, dark hair and a pale complexion quickly step to the side before the double doors of the saloon swung shut.

Stifling a curse, Bowen was on the move, determination making him fast even as resignation flooded his body. The night couldn't get much worse, and now he was about to tangle with a drunk woman, and hand Beck a prime opportunity to make an ass of himself as he pleaded mea culpa. Hopefully he could get drunk bridesmaid home without having to wash and detail the inside of his truck—again. Not enough Febreze in Monroes' grocery store or Big Z's Hardware to get that smell out. He knew from bitter experience that rarely did a good deed go unpunished.

Bowen pushed open the doors and supported the woman as she teetered on her high heels, and clung to Beck, nearly tumbling him to the sidewalk.

"Thanks," Beck said, his stricken gaze immediately glued on Ashni.

"Evening," Bowen tipped his hat to both women as Beck just gaped—flushed, and dismayed. Ash should have been his sister-in-law years ago, but something had kept Beck balancing on that deteriorating fence.

She should have kicked his ass to the curb. Ring or move on.

Bowen had never seen her look so angry.

And hurt.

Damn.

"I got it from here," Bowen said and disentangled the woman's octopus hold on Beck.

Ashni's narrowed eyes—a beautiful obsidian—sparked fury, and even Bowen felt burned.

Ouch, he mouthed to Beck, who'd already taken a step toward Ashni, arms out, face apologetic, clearly going into soothing mode, which suited him far more than troublemaker or womanizer ever would.

"I'll get…ah…" Bowen looked down into the woman's upturned face. She might be pretty. Hard to tell with that much makeup and her unfocused stare.

"Shauna," Beck said quickly. "I think, or maybe Shannon?"

Great. So now what? He was going to have to get her in his truck and rummage through her purse. Well, couldn't be helped. And it wasn't as if Beck were to blame.

Again, the no good deed goes unpunished theme played in his head.

"Hey, you're cute," the woman said, a delicate hand reaching up to cup his face. "A cowboy. I did get me a cowboy. I said I would. Wait." She stood up more fully. Tall. Slim. But curved in all the right places—and pretty obvious about it.

Too bad she couldn't hold her liquor.

"Are you the same cowboy?" she blinked. Wide, blue eyes.

But not whiskey colored.

Where the heck had that come from?

Shauna or Shannon was the buzzed one. Not him. He'd never even got a sip of that whiskey, he thought regretfully. And his earlier beer had remained untouched. Bodhi's fault. Fate's fault.

"You look sorta the same."

He, Bodhi and Beck could easily pass for brothers. They were closer than many brothers he'd met over the years.

"Doesn't matter," Bowen said, a little amused, but also sad.

She could be a really nice person, but why'd she feel the need to get so wasted? And where were her friends? Someone thought enough of her to invite her to stand up with them at their wedding, but not enough to make sure she didn't get plastered? Or if she did, that she got home safe?

"Let me take you home, ma'am." He tipped his head rather than his hat because his arms were full. She was strong.

No wonder Beck, who easily controlled bucking broncs, had struggled. But Bowen rode bulls. And he often won.

"I love the ma'am thing. It's just like a cowboy romance novel." Shauna or Shannon sighed. "This is the wrong way. My room is down there." She gestured the other way down Main Street as Bowen practically carried her toward his truck.

"At the big hotel. Sorta fancy. Wow, that's a lotta stars. Don't see those like that in Seattle. Or cowboys. I'm moving."

"So you're visiting. You staying at the Graff?"

The Graff was one of the nicest historic hotels in the West. It had been saved and remodeled by Cormac Sheenan a handful of years ago. Judging by Shauna/Shannon's dress, shoes and handbag—the label of which he recognized, as his mother only thought top-shelf everything would suit her—Shauna/Shannon was all about appearances. His mother claimed it was to exude success so that her clients felt comfortable. But even when reading at home by the fire, his mom often slipped into a Chanel jacket or Gucci something. Her clothes were those most people only saw in magazines, and she also had no reservations telling him exactly what she wanted for her birthday, Mother's Day and Christmas, so Bowen knew how much that shit cost.

"That's it," Shauna/Shannon said. "And I got a nice room. Not a suite though, but the bed's pretty. And I bet comfortable especially for a big man like you, not that I imagine we're going to do much sleeping." She slipped her arm around his waist and leaned into him.

True. They wouldn't be sleeping—not together. Hopefully she'd get some shut-eye as she was going to have a doozy of a hangover. And he doubted he'd get any sleep after his grandfather's announcement and the subsequent challenge Bodhi had drop-kicked into his and Beck's teeth.

Get engaged? Hell, he didn't even have a date to the Saturday night steak dinner.

And he'd never had a woman cheering him on in the stands, but he'd had his share of opportunities to indulge over his career. Many women lined up for autographs or showed up at sponsor parties or the sponsor bar after the rodeo looking for a good time. So he wasn't worried about getting a date.

But a bride?

Bowen started thinking about women he knew in Marietta. He'd spent summers here growing up. Holidays. He came back on most tour breaks to help his granddad with the ranch.

This is dumb.

He could hardly call an old acquaintance and ask them for a favor. Laughably awkward. Someone local from a family his granddad knew might be more believable but could potentially cause more heartache. It would feel even more like a lie.

Shauna or Shannon hummed. He quickly walked the few blocks to the Graff and practically carried her up through the front entrance, hoping he could somehow retrieve her room key from her fire-engine-red clutch. She smiled up at him and draped her arms around his neck.

"I'm on the second floor," she said helpfully and with surprising strength lifted herself up so that he had no choice but to scoop her fully into his arms. She leaned back and laughed and began to sing a Lizzo song about a new man and a Minnesota football player.

That was at least unexpected. She had a good, although slurred, tone. Good pitch.

He crossed the lobby, gaining more than a few smirks. A beautiful bartender with long, white-blonde hair in some kind of fancy braid caught his eye.

"I'll send up some seltzer water with lemon and lime and a wedge of candied ginger. It will help," she said. "Which room?"

Hell if he knew. Might as well go full white knight and get the drunk princess to her bed and bring her a glass of doctored water. Maybe the bartender would even spot him an aspirin.

"I'll come back down and get it."

He took the stairs two at a time.

"You are strong," she cooed.

He may not have grown up full time on Three Tree Ranch, but he was rodeo and ranch-work ripped.

"It's like we're married and you're carrying me over the threshold. So romantic." And then, because Bowen's luck with women often sucked, she began to sob.

"Problem, cowboy?" The husky voice stopped him in his

tracks.

A petite woman, two stairs ahead of him, blocked his path. Her lush, full lips mocked his predicament, and because she was staring down at him, Bowen found himself in the unusual position of having to look up at a woman.

The eyes hit him—crinkled in the corners in amusement and a rich amber like his favorite whiskey. Familiar, and yet no name rattled out from the past to help him.

"You don't remember me." Her gaze cooled a fraction and at the same time challenged.

Dammit. He hadn't slept with her, right? He would have remembered that. And he never played in Marietta because, well, small town and one he hoped to settle in the moment he could get his cousins to retire from the rodeo and put down the roots they'd always talked about.

Here.

Montana.

Three Tree Ranch.

And all that might be in jeopardy now.

"Ummmmmm," he delayed. "It's been a while. How you doing?"

Her nostrils flared; she clearly wasn't buying his half-assed stall. She tossed her head as if a mane of hair would bounce around her shoulders, but her short, sleek mannish bob stuck like a helmet. Still, the movement triggered something in his brain.

"Bowen Ballantyne," she said, clearly at an advantage. "You fixing to break another girl's heart tonight?"

Chapter Two

DID THE UNIVERSE have it out for her or what? In one month—this past July, which was now the month of woe and disaster and should be struck from the calendar forever for obvious reasons—Langston Carr had lost her fiancé to betrayal, her job to spite, her earnest money on a downtown Missoula townhouse to greed, and then an even more deeply personal loss she wouldn't let herself think about. Except she couldn't stop thinking about it.

And now, because she'd been desperate for income, she'd accepted a year-long gig as an event planner in her former hometown where her family had generated more than its fair share of gossip and scandal over the generations. When she'd left for college and her grandfather had sold off the last of his struggling ranch, leaving her with no home to return to, Langston had thought she'd kissed Marietta goodbye forever.

Not so easy.

And then, just to kick her when she was down and spit in her face, what did fate do? The mocking bitch laughed and decreed that the first event she would be supervising at the historic Graff Hotel was her wedding—or would have been hers. Same date. Same flowers. Same venue. Same cake.

Same touristy events planned for the prestigious out-of-town wedding guests. Same groom and controlling, wealthy, and ambitious family. Different dress. Different bride.

And who was the lucky lady marrying into one of Montana's wealthiest, most politically connected families? Her cousin. Her lying, cheating and flaunting it pregnant cousin!

Langston thought the turn her life had taken couldn't suck any more, but no. Tonight fate laughed and did a Beyoncé-worthy hair toss as if snarking at her, "Hey, girl, it can always get worse. Let me show you."

Here stood the bane of her childhood and dreamy teen years. Gray-blue eyes. Bone structure straight off a romance novel cover: firm, determined mouth, wide shoulders, rangy body, ranch and cowboy cut muscles encased in worn Wranglers. His western-style shirt was open at his strong, tanned throat, and the sleeves were rolled up carelessly to mid forearm.

Langston couldn't breathe.

She couldn't swallow.

And the arrogant bastard didn't even remember her.

Would she get fired if she slapped him? He'd probably remember her then.

And he wasn't a hotel guest. He must be in town for the Copper Mountain Rodeo next weekend, so he'd be staying at the Three Tree Ranch with his granddad, Ben Ballantyne.

Langston drew back from the brink. Her savings had been fully depleted on the townhouse down payment, where now her ex and his new bride were going to live. And he may or may not pay her back. Looked like court and lawyer fees were in her future.

So a slap might relieve her feelings, but no. She was a professional, and no matter how many times life knocked her down, she was going to pop back up, brush the dirt off her backside and mount up again like the cowgirl she'd once been.

But dang, it was hard some days.

It was just one more insult in a summer of them. In August, she'd let herself grieve. September was her rebuilding month. She was halfway through and back on her feet. Sort of.

"Sorry." She let her insincerity shine. "Didn't mean to interrupt your drunken booty call." Dramatically she stepped to one side of the beautifully restored staircase and expansively motioned for him to continue on up.

"This is not what it appears to be, ma'am," Bowen said even as Shauna pressed kisses along his superb jawline.

Ma'am. Ever the cowboy. But it made her feel eighty. Since the losses had piled up, she had felt like she'd aged a handful of decades in a couple of painful months.

Ahhhh, shoot. Now she was being mean, and she didn't want to be that girl. Bitter. Sad. Angry. Not her style before, and she wasn't going to let heartache and disappointment turn her into a bitter person—like her mom and her granddaddy.

She dug deep for a smile, but her pockets were empty.

"You staying at the Graff?" he asked, and she could hear

the hope in his voice. He neatly dodged Shauna's wandering hands as she reached for his belt buckle.

It didn't look new. And Langston didn't want to be caught staring, but of course she wondered which rodeo he'd won that buckle at. Bowen had been hella skilled as a teen; she could only imagine what a decade plus had added to his skill stable.

"I work here."

"Perfect," Bowen said. His gray-blue eyes lit up making him so potently handsome that her breath caught.

Her fingers flexed and she pressed her palms to her practical gray skirt. Shauna was already climbing on him. Another man lost to her overtly sexy cousins.

You never had Bowen. Ever.

And that rejection, though years ago, still stung.

"Maybe you can help me out." He angled his hero's jaw out of Shauna's lips' target practice range but jiggled her to share his meaning.

"No thank you. Too kinky for me," she deadpanned. And then stared in fascination as a faint pink stained the knife-edge of his cheekbones, which really belonged in a cologne ad.

What would his fragrance be?

"What? No. We're not…I'm just…I'm not even sure of her name," he said, his cheeks staining to red now, and for the first time in nearly two months, Langston laughed.

"Am I supposed to be impressed that you usually ask their name first?"

That gorgeous jaw gritted, and he looked so hot. Now that she had most of his attention, Langston wanted to irritate him more.

"You have this all wrong." Bowen's voice dropped to gravel.

But for the first time in months, Langston felt like something was right.

"Tell me how," she said, her voice innocent. Oh boy, when he realized who she was, he was going to feel all kinds of stupid. If he remembered. She cut off that depressing thought.

"She was at Grey's. Part of a bridal party." Bowen's low voice had always sounded like a muted race car engine idling, which, when she'd been a teen, had made something rev up deep inside of her. Unfortunately, Bowen hadn't talked all that much, and he and his cousins had only been in Marietta for summers.

"Thought I'd help her back to her room. Make sure she comes to no harm."

Of course Bowen would take care of a woman who cut loose and wandered a bit too far out of her lane. He was built that way. Old-school cowboy. A good man. Cue sappy music. She could feel the sigh build up in her soul.

Get over it.

He wouldn't cheat on his fiancée, especially after… She shut down that thought, but she could practically hear the attic door of her brain where she stuffed all the scary and painful detritus of her life creak open a crack.

"Follow me," she said.

"Thank you, ma'am."

"Ma'am, my ass," Langston said, taking the clutch purse that rested on Shauna's stomach now that Bowen had picked her up. She fished through it for the key and then plopped the clutch back on Shauna's washboard-flat tummy a little harder than necessary. Pilates queen.

"Ouch, runt," Shauna called out and then laughed and began singing again.

"Even drunk Shauna's in tune. We used to do karaoke battles, and she was always my biggest competition."

Langston couldn't help the bitter spurt. They may not have grown up together as cousins or been terribly close, but Shauna could have warned her that her twin was poaching.

But Mason had been happy to be bagged and tagged.

"You know her?"

"Cousin."

"Then why aren't you at the party?"

Why was Bowen Ballantyne getting nosy?

Ignoring that fraught question, Langston hurried up the rest of the flight of stairs before Shauna got to the belting part of the song.

"You know it's bad when she's singing Lizzo," Langston said conversationally. "I warned you about the pink drinks," she scolded her cousin. "Grey's is notorious for them, and Jason Grey always has a heavy hand pouring for the bridal groups. Probably revenge."

"That's a little harsh."

Langston paused in the act of sliding the key into the lock. She'd heard the story about Jason Grey—how his wife had left him and his daughters years ago. Was he still bitter? She'd always thought he'd been justified. But she didn't want to drive down that road and close herself off to happiness. Another man shouldn't get heat for her dad's lifestyle and her fiancé's choices.

She unlocked the door.

"Drop her on the bed," she told Bowen, trying and failing to not stare at his ass in his Wranglers. She would not objectify a man. She was done with men for a while. But the way Bowen's western-style shirt fit and the flex of his shoulders as he leaned over to deposit a clinging Shauna was out of a movie. Only real. No lighting or photoshopping necessary. And the way his Wranglers hugged his butt and thighs might as well be a magnet and her gaze metal.

Just because she was back in Marietta, she was not going to get swoony over a cowboy. Even *the* cowboy—the fantasy cowboy from her teen dreams. Sheesh! She was older, wiser and…and…he didn't even remember her.

"You are not going to watch us, runt." Shauna struggled to sit up.

"There will be nothing to watch," Langston informed her breezily and didn't look at Bowen. "You need to get some sleep, or you won't be feeling well tomorrow. And you've got the hiking and zip-line excursion starting at ten."

"Let's get this off. Oooooh, this is a real buckle. A real cowboy buckle." Shauna grabbed tight to Bowen's belt, jerking him down toward her. "You ride bulls—let's see how well you ride me." She worked to get the buckle off.

Langston clapped her hand over Shauna's mouth and pulled her other wandering hand away from Bowen's southern regions. "Run while you can, cowboy. I got this. Or she might snag something even more important to you."

How was it possible that Bowen Ballantyne, All-Around Cowboy and one of the best bull riders on the pro rodeo circuit, was blushing? He probably swept women off their feet every night. They probably got drunk off of all the pheromones he emitted like a homing beacon.

"She going to be all right?"

"Did you get her drunk?" Langston shouldn't have asked that. Shauna loved a good time, and any responsibility would be hers. She often one-night standed it and had zero regrets the next day. Heck, she posted her conquests.

"Of course not." He sounded offended. Langston had to remind herself to look away as he redid his belt buckle. Copper Mountain. All-Around Cowboy, 2009. And why was she riveted anywhere near his belt or below it? One would wager she'd have gained some subtlety after a decade plus of no Bowen sightings except on the internet.

One would lose that bet.

She jerked her eyes north to see a faint smile light his mouth. Now she was the one blushing. She waved her fingers at the door.

"Time to run, cowboy. It's what you do best."

"Where the hell did that come from?" Bowen demanded,

looking at her more closely, clearly racking his brain for how he knew her and what he'd done to piss her off.

Dang her and her big mouth. Did she want him to remember her? Had she really changed that much? Had she really been so unmemorable?

She'd given him the out he clearly needed. Why wasn't he taking it? Now he could go back to the bar and his cousins and the buckle bunnies who were probably lining up to find the cowboy they were going to try to snag for rodeo weekend. True, it was a little early, but early bird got the worm and all that.

He would be one more man she would try to avoid this coming week from hell.

"What did I do in the past to piss you off so fierce?"

"Nothing." Her voice sounded as deflated as she felt.

She was being a bitch. She didn't want to be a bitch. She closed her eyes trying to summon something—patience, peace of mind, perkiness.

When she opened them and straightened her spine and her shoulders like she had before mounting Buttercup to head into the arena, Shauna had kicked off her shoes and was wiggling out of her dress.

"Just go," Langston urged because he was taking up all the air in the room. She could smell him, feel his energy. "You've done your good deed. I'll take it from here."

"The bartender downstairs made a special drink for her. Said it helps with hangovers."

"Shane. Of course she would do that."

"How about I bring that up and then leave."

"Thanks." Langston waited for the lock's snick.

Instead she heard the soft, careful footfalls of worn leather sole on wood.

"Your eyes," he said, his voice a whisper behind her. "They're familiar, but we don't know each other. Do we?"

"You really don't remember, do you?" She turned around, holding herself stiffly so she wouldn't do something infinitely stupid like press herself against all that hard, hot, masculine cowboy.

"Did we…? Did I…?" He stopped.

The silence clawed at her, alive, hungry.

She could practically feel the heat from his body, and the urge to lean into him and pull from his strength and kindness nearly overwhelmed her. She just felt so raw. Stripped. Vulnerable in a way she never thought she'd be.

"I've been dismissed a lot," she admitted. She kept her chin high. "But I never thought I was totally forgettable."

But her father had seemed to forget about her. Over. And over. Her mom had walked. Her grandpa had sold up and left. And Mason hadn't kept her in mind when he'd jumped ship for more fertile pastures.

"Jesus," Bowen breathed, his voice soft like a prayer, and maybe they could both use one right about now. "I'm a jerk. I've heard that a lot," he said. "From more than a few women, but I'd never forget a woman who gifted me—"

Langston huffed a laugh. "Get off your high horse and stuff the flowery language, cowboy. Totally doesn't suit."

Thank God her temper had finally kicked in. His hotness now irked her. "I'm probably the only woman in town you haven't euphemistically slept with."

He stared at her, his gray-blue eyes puzzled, his brain ticking over and over like the rainbow ball of doom on her last MacBook Air that she'd finally had to replace.

"Ummmmm…I'm sorry?"

"You should be. You missed a great opportunity. A fantastic one. I'm epic in bed."

Said nobody ever to her. Bowen hadn't been the only boy to reject her advances. And her two so-called college boyfriends hadn't texted back after she'd dredged up her confidence and finally let them get her horizontal. And then there'd been Mason. Her fiancé. Three years with him only to catch him a couple of months before their wedding acrobatically banging her cousin in the king-size bed she'd bought for after their wedding.

But that was the past. And in the future she was going to find a spectacular, adventurous lover and blow his mind.

"Good to know." He tipped his hat and smiled, and she scolded her susceptible heart, which needed to be locked away for a couple of years—make that decades. Sexy lovers, yes, falling in love, no.

"And now that you've informed me of all I missed over the years, why don't you introduce yourself properly."

Now he pulled out the charm? Langston crossed her arms and cocked her hip. Shauna softly snored.

"Langston Carr."

"Dandelion?"

"Have all cowboys in Marietta lost their touch?" she demanded.

"I haven't."

Langston was shocked by the flare of heat those words lit. She needed to douse that fast. Adventurous lover, yes. Bowen Ballantyne, no. No. No. No.

"I think you have. Women don't want to be reminded of their stupid childhood nicknames. I've matured. I'm a woman now. Professional."

"I can see that," Bowen said, and his eyes took a slow walk over her corporate attire that fired up her nerves and made her self-control slip. "Still, Dandy suited at the time."

"So that's why you wrapped me up in your denim jacket and tossed me out of your truck like you were trying to escape a grenade."

His eyes widened at the memory. "I was. You were sixteen!"

The rejection had hurt.

And maybe it was dumb to bring it up, but Langston was tired of everyone else getting the last say.

"Lang," he began.

"Langston," she said with dignity. Her mother had been a creative free spirit and had named her after her favorite poet, Langston Hughes. The name was all she had left of her mother. Not even any specific memories. She'd tired of motherhood, ranch life, and waiting for her bull-riding, gambling lover to come home before Langston had hit three.

"Langston," he corrected and then that cool, assessing gaze walked over her like he was at a livestock auction. "How the hell was I supposed to recognize you? What have you done to your hair?"

Reflexively she reached for her sheared head. Yes, it was horrible. But she'd wanted to make a statement. About what, had been lost in translation. But her cropped hair did indicate the direction her life would now take. Serious. Professional. Disciplined.

"Good to see you too, Bowen." His name sounded like a curse, and that made her feel a little better. "No wonder Bodhi always got the girls."

Langston couldn't take it anymore. The fantasy of her youth had definitely crashed into the reality of her present, and the drunk, amorous traitor Shauna was better company than a cowboy who really should keep his opinions about her appearance to himself.

"Go," she ordered. "Just go. And keep your mouth shut on your way out."

Dang, but he was stupid hot. Stupid beautiful. And just plain stupid.

She opened the hotel room door, kept it open with her foot, and then propelled him out into the hall, trying to *not* notice that his obliques felt like glacier stones carved by eons of wind and water.

"Consider me one more woman who thinks you're a jerk. You should get a life-size poster made that we can sell in the hotel's gift shop so women can enjoy the eye candy without the critique!" She slammed the door, barely missing his prime ass. Too bad, too, because a bruised ass would make his bull riding this weekend even more painful.

She leaned against the door and caught her reflection in the mirror above the antique writing desk. Langston pulled at the corners of her mouth and stuck out her tongue, feeling slightly better.

"I bet he'll remember me now."

WHAT JUST HAPPENED?

Bowen stared at the door that still seemed to be rattling with unrepressed rage—an exclamation point to the whole odd encounter.

Lang Carr. Fierce barrel racer. Big mouth. Big heart. Bigger attitude. Tiny girl, and she hadn't grown much above five feet from what he could tell. But what she'd lacked in size she'd more than made up for in quick, deadly wit, riding skills and a will to win. She might have tried to tame her hair, but her mouth wasn't any less subdued.

Not that he hadn't deserved her ire.

Most of the kids on the summer teen local rodeo circuit thought Bodhi had nicknamed her, but, unfortunately, it had been him. He'd gone out with his granddad and cousins to talk to her grandpa about buying a few horses and, he learned later, land. Lang had been balancing on one of the corral fences. Her normally braided hair had been loose—a wild, white-blonde mass of curls streaming behind her and dancing in the breeze. He'd murmured she looked like a dandelion, and Bodhi had grinned, and Bowen had known then that he'd doomed the poor girl. He must have been about twelve, old enough to know better.

"Well, hell." He hesitated outside the door, unsure what to do.

He might not sweet-talk women, but when he did open his mouth, he didn't usually insert both boots. He'd never had the gift of charm like Bodhi, and when Bodhi messed up, nearly everyone instantly forgave him. Bodhi radiated charisma like asphalt radiated heat in late July. Bowen had to work to gain attention or forgiveness.

He headed toward the wide staircase. So Dandy...little Lang was back in Marietta, and again pissed off at him. Probably better that way. He should let this go. He'd likely tangle any fence-mending attempt with her. And it's not like they could build a friendship or something else. Local women had always been off the table, but, damn, she still had the most beautiful eyes of any woman he'd ever met. Large, widely spaced and the color of whiskey. They'd always seemed lit from within as if she had so much life inside of her—like it was a flame.

And then there had been her hair that had crackled with just as much attitude and beauty. She'd been the most alive person, other than her dad and Bodhi, that he'd ever met. Her hair had danced around her face and flowed down her back like a flag of independence heralding her untamed spirit.

Why the hell had she cut it? It was as if she'd doused her inner fire. And he was thinking about her way too much.

Still, he hesitated before turning away and taking the stairs.

"Might as well have mentioned the loss of her freckles while you were at it, dumbass," he mumbled.

Lang was well rid of him, but he could make her life a bit easier if he brought up the doctored water the bartender had promised. There were still several couples sitting in the pub-style bar, but the vibe was so different from Grey's. The bartender would rake in the tips at Grey's, but she'd also get a barn full of dumb cowboys spewing what they thought were their best lines. And Jason would get a lot of batting practice in—if he still kept his bat behind the bar.

"Ready for the elixir?"

The bartender was striking, and her eyes were a beautiful, almost mystical aquamarine color, but he couldn't drop-kick Lang's delicate features, voluptuous mouth and stunning eyes out of his mind.

"And an aspirin if you have it," he said. "I just hope Lang can get some of this down her. She was already dozing off."

"Langston?" she queried. "She just started working here this week. You must be friends already. I'm Shane," she said casually as she filled up a glass with seltzer water and then garnished it with two slices of lemon and lime and a few herbs. She sliced some candied ginger and stuck it on the side of the glass.

"Get her to chew on the ginger if you can," she said. "It will help with the nausea."

"I'm just the messenger," he said. "I'm hoping Lang can handle it."

"I only met Langston today." She stressed the name. "And that quick hello gave me the impression she can handle anything."

She grinned cheekily and handed him a plate with the drink on a cocktail napkin, along with a few artfully arranged crackers with a pat of butter. Then she handed him a bowl. "Just in case."

"You've thought of everything."

"It's my job."

Bowen took the hangover helper back upstairs, and with each step, his mind turned on the puzzle that was Langston today: Why was she back in Marietta? Why wasn't she enjoying her cousin's bachelorette party? And why did she look so somber?

He tried and failed to suppress the vivid teenage memory of Lang running across the dirt parking lot after most of the rigs had pulled out. Her hair had streamed behind her like a living cloud. She'd worn a short, flowered denim miniskirt, red cowboy boots and a white western shirt with red piping. She'd already been unbuttoning the shirt when she'd jumped on his truck's running board, her budding cleavage and soft pink bra deliberately visible through his open window.

Had he hurt her feelings by jumping out of his truck, covering her up in his jacket and then pulling out again in a cloud of dust? He'd been in college. If he hadn't removed her from his truck's runner, likely he would have been marched to the sheriff's office on the business end of a shotgun.

He hesitated outside of the door. Langston hadn't seemed in the mood for an apology. But he wasn't in the mood to head back to Grey's and watch Bodhi work his magic on some unsuspecting tourist or Beck's mea culpa with Ashni. And if he headed back to the ranch, he'd only stew about his grandfather's bomb. He'd already tried talking to him about it—hanging back when the others had headed to Grey's. Stubborn man.

Bowen knew all about that trait.

Feeling on edge, he lightly rapped on the door. It was hard to reconcile the small, mouthy barrel racer with the spark-filled eyes with the subdued woman in a gray suit and corporate cut, looking like she was about to launch a hostile takeover.

A deeply unimpressed Langston Carr, hands on her hips, stood before him.

"Room service too? What other skills have you been hiding, cowboy?"

The possibilities raced through his head.

He leaned against the doorjamb in a move he'd seen Bodhi do a million times. Worked for him, and Bowen was dumb to jack his cousin's moves, but he was going to need all the help he could get.

Chapter Three

"Bowen. Not cowboy."

Her eye roll was nearly audible.

"If you want me to call you Langston—all those syllables—then you can call me Bowen."

"Cowboy is two syllables. Same as Bo-wen." She clapped it out and to his total shock his dick stirred. "And who's to say I'll be needing your name all that much?"

There she is.

Something inside of him rose up in response. It felt alive, almost like he had to lasso it and call it back.

But Langston was Marietta. He shouldn't be attracted to her.

Shauna mumbled behind Langston.

"Give her the drink and let's get out of here."

"Where?"

He hadn't thought that part out. He hadn't even planned on issuing an invitation.

She took the offering and looked suspiciously at the glass. "I heard Shane has a cure to stave off hangovers. Headaches too. I'm going to need that recipe after this long week," he heard her mutter as she left to wake Shauna enough to down the drink and eat a couple of the crackers with the butter and ginger.

He used his boot to keep the door open.

Langston returned, duty done—Shauna lying back down again, cuddled up in the big bed.

"Take a walk with me," he urged.

"Why?"

"I got to have a reason?"

"It's been twelve years since you tossed my ass in the dirt, Bowen." She turned to face him, eyes sparking and her creamy skin glowing in the low light of the room.

Ahhhh. There were the freckles.

"Don't even try to pull out some of the famous Ballantyne charm at this late date."

"That charm skipped me and went straight to Bodhi, giving him a double dose."

"Can't argue there. Bodhi could charm a charging bison."

"Ouch for stampeding bison everywhere." Bowen found himself smiling. "Take a walk with me."

"You snagged plenty of that charm," Lang groused. "Don't give me the innocent act. Why do you want to go for a walk with me?"

"Dang, girl, you are suspicious," he drawled and this time he felt a slow burn low in his body that heated him up. He smiled real slow like he'd seen Bodhi do a million times to get himself or one of them out of trouble. Only, of course, it didn't work for him.

Lang huffed out a breath and went to run her fingers through her hair but stopped herself. She must have only had it cut recently.

"You and Bodhi got some kind of a game going on? Role switching or something?"

That hit too close to home.

Lang assessed him, much like he'd seen her do to her competition at the teen rodeos. Despite his best intentions, Bowen's competitive spirit rose. He wanted her to take a walk with him. He wanted to get back in her good graces.

He straightened against the doorjamb. She'd likely shut him down, but if you never played, you never won.

"It's a beautiful night. I want some company," he admitted. "And maybe grovel a bit."

"This I have to see." Langston moved toward him, close enough that he imagined he felt the brush of her breasts against his arm. "I want to change out of this suit first before you get on your knees, Bowen."

She smirked and strode past him. Bowen had to do a quick adjust before he followed, letting the door close behind him. Lang walked down the hall, full of purpose, and Bowen found himself fascinated by her fluid exit and the sexy AF swish of her hips.

✪

"DUMB. THIS IS dumb." Langston zipped up her Wranglers and pulled her flowered crop T-shirt over her head. As she stomped her feet into her well-worn red boots to match the red and orange poppies decorating her stretchy off-the-shoulder T, she couldn't help the quick look in the mirror.

God. Her hair. When would she get used to it? And why had she thought chopping it all off would solve her problems? It was like she was a cursed, hapless beauty in a Greek myth, only she'd wreaked vengeance on herself with no jealous, vengeful Hera in sight.

Langston resisted the temptation to wet her hair to get the sticky gel out. If she did that, the curls would spring back, and this tight to her head that would be a full embrace of her childhood nickname.

She glared at her reflection. She shouldn't care. She really shouldn't. She wasn't trying to impress Bowen Ballantyne. Tried that. And it had taken months to get through a day without the flare of humiliation. And even longer to screw up her courage to date in college and have confidence in a man's desire—which had once again been tossed back in her face. Thrown over for her shallow, statuesque, and breast-enhanced cousin.

She stuck her tongue out again at herself. She had to create her own happy. No man was going to do that. Her so-called father and grandpa had proven that. Mason had given her a stark reminder.

Lesson learned, boys. She was going to not only survive this week at the Graff, she was going to thrive. And she'd be a brilliant event planner this year. She might no longer have a ranch to call home or be a rising teen rodeo star, but she still had some cowgirl sass.

She liked the sound her boots made on the restored hardwood floor of the lobby. The *click-thunk* resonated with confidence. And she needed that because tonight she was going to vanquish the ghost of Bowen Ballantyne forever.

Bowen waited by the gift shop next to a half-sized distressed metals statue of a cowboy on a bucking bronc that he could have modeled for. Owner Miranda Telford had already closed for the night.

"There you are," he murmured, tossing her out of the saddle of the conversation before she'd fully mounted as she saw the way his gaze swept over her body. The jeans, boots and T-shirt suddenly felt far more revealing than her business suit had.

She'd ditched the western staples when she'd started her internship at Mason's mother's event planning company her last year of college. She'd needed to impress clients and earn the trust of her colleagues. The new style had hammered home that she wasn't a ranch kid or a cowgirl anymore. So why had she impulsively brought back her old Wranglers and boots?

"Where shall we go?" she asked trying to ignore how good he looked. If only she could borrow Bowen Ballantyne for a few strategic moments of arm candy at the Graff over the next handful of days until the wedding was over. That would be a saucy middle finger to Mason, his mom, and her cousins.

Bowen meeting her after work, smiling down into her

upturned face and laughing at some of her jokes before he'd cup her face and…sheesh! She needed to stop her late-night obsessive romance reading because she couldn't sleep. But if she could parade Bowen around town a bit—have him show up at the hotel before or after the tightly scheduled wedding events happened, it would show her former fiancé, his family and her former colleagues that not only had she moved on, she'd moved *on*!

Bowen would make all the women who'd been so smug and fake-sympathetic to her gnash their teeth in envy.

And I really should be more mature than this.

"What are you thinking?" he asked.

"What? Why?" Had she been looking particularly vindictive?

"The walk."

Whew. She waved at Bob at the front desk and Shane at the bar. A few of her former colleagues sat at one of the tables nibbling on appetizers and drinking one of Shane's specialty cocktails. They stopped mid-conversation and stared.

Brilliant.

She spun around so that she was flush with Bowen's chest. She smiled up at him and allowed her fingers to almost brush against the snaps on his shirt. He looked a bit shocked at her change in attitude, but since he was facing her, and not the bar, it was no big deal.

She laughed and slipped her arm though his, and Bowen was too much of an old-fashioned cowboy to object—just like she'd known he would be.

"What would you suggest?" She let her smile go full wattage as she shifted so that her expression could be seen at the bar. She could practically feel the stares boring into Bowen's back.

Watch and weep, ladies.

She stepped a little away from him, letting her hand run along the length of his arm. Dang. Felt like stone, and her tummy flipped. She was pretending—putting on a show, not trying to fall under her own fiction.

"Oops." She deliberately dropped her small, leather backpack-style purse.

Bowen picked it up and slid the straps over her shoulder, leaning down to nuzzle her neck.

"We putting on a show for some reason?" His voice was a sexy whisper that slid down her spine and spread like sun-warmed honey through her body. "Not that I object in any way."

"Yes, please," she choked out, her voice unrecognizable.

Bowen slowly straightened and looked down into her face. His eyes were clear and direct and the color of the sky just before dawn broke. She couldn't breathe as his intense regard stretched out. Then he cupped her jaw and let his work-hardened thumb feather along her now slamming pulse.

He lowered his head with impossible slowness, and Langston felt like her heart was going to jump out of her body and strut down Main Street. His lips parted. He hesitated a beat and then another. The tension—would he or wouldn't he kiss her?—clawed to get out. She stood on her toes so she could kiss him. But he still held her jaw, so instead of a quick peck, his lips brushed with infinite tenderness across hers back and forth. She could barely feel his touch—more like the promise of one.

Better than any romance novel ever.

He broke the kiss, and his lips tilted into the ghost of a smile.

"Good enough?"

"And some." Her voice shook, and she realized she was clutching his arms like she was drowning, and he was a tree branch growing out along the Marietta riverbank.

Bowen reached around her and opened the hotel's doors and then with one arm around her waist, he walked her out into the night.

What just happened?

I kissed Bowen Ballantyne.

Her limbs felt like they couldn't coordinate.

"You want to share what that spectacle was all about?"

She pressed her still-tingling lips together to keep her fingers from touching them, savoring the feel of his mouth against hers. Mason had never made her feel breathless or dizzy or like her body was going to fly apart.

"You mind?" She tried to gauge his mood.

"Happy to oblige."

She laughed. "Then thank you for the best assist ever, Bowen."

"The best," he repeated.

Way to overstroke his ego. She probably should explain, but he wouldn't demand it. And she'd look petty and insecure. Besides, it wasn't like they were friends and would be spending more time together. Tonight was a stolen adventure, but if her intention had been to flirt or tease and slay the dragon of her Bowen Ballantyne crush into oblivion, that had been a dumb start.

"So, where shall we walk?" She wanted to distract him from what had happened in the lobby. Heck, she needed to distract herself.

"Want to walk through the park and to the fairgrounds?" Bowen caught up to her in two long-legged strides. "Lotta memories for you there."

Her step hitched along with her breath.

Of course he'd want to go there. Other than his granddaddy's Three Tree Ranch, where else would a cowboy want to go in town? She'd only been back in Marietta a week, and she'd avoided the fairgrounds. And horses. And her childhood memories until Bowen strolled back into her life.

"You've got your horse stabled there already?"

"No. Drove home to the ranch tonight," he said. "We'll move our horses over Thursday or Friday."

We. His cousins. Bodhi and Beckett. It had always been like that. The three of them. She'd always wanted siblings. She'd had cousins. And they'd been friendly as kids, but once the teen years had hit along with more financial trouble, her cousins had moved to Missoula, and the relationship had frayed. She hadn't realized how badly until a few months ago.

Without really agreeing, they walked along Main Street, which was pretty quiet now. The windows of the shops were already decorated for the rodeo—some had hay bales outside with faux mini corrals built to house the sidewalk sales during rodeo weekend. Painted wood or cardboard cutouts of horses cattle and cowboys were propped in the windows, and many of the windows had ranch or rodeo scenes painted.

"The decorations are even more elaborate than when we were kids," she chatted, too nervous to let the silence settle between them. "There's a contest between merchants. Friendly. No prize. Just bragging rights."

He nodded.

Right. The quiet Ballantyne.

Why should she help him out by making conversation? She'd wanted peace with her past—and to truly move on after the past painful few months. What better way to face it than with the penultimate cowboy at her side?

"There were no decorations in the Graff."

He noticed. That had not been in her wedding agenda. "The bridal party is using most of the hotel for the wedding and wedding activities," she said, thinking it must sound horribly arrogant to Bowen, who seemed to be the epitome of a down-to-earth cowboy, and yet he came from a huge established ranch. He was a top competitor and one of the top earners annually on the pro rodeo circuit.

"They are a politically connected family, state and federal, and quite wealthy." She tried to keep her voice neutral. "There will be some interviews and scenes shot for a future campaign bio video."

"Why the Graff then?"

That had been her idea, wanting to get married in her hometown. Mason's father had loved the quaint roots and the whole heritage Montana theme. It would make his city-raised, Ivy League-educated son seem more of a down-home Montana man when he ran for senate. And she had inadvertently helped them weave this homespun tale that was mostly a lie.

"It's a beautiful hotel. Cormac Sheenan put a lot of money and research into doing it right. It's a beautiful backdrop and a charming town. Lots of recreational activities for the guests."

"You sound like a commercial."

"Event planner."

They crossed to the park in front of the courthouse. The dark green grass was just too inviting, and, impulsively, Langston kicked off her boots, peeled off her socks and let the soles of her feet just absorb the cool and soft and green. It had been a long and emotional day toward the end of a long, painful summer. But she would get through it. One day at a time. Just one more week, and then she'd do her best to put Mason and his family and her losses forever in her rearview mirror.

Langston tilted her head back to savor the peek-a-boo view of the star-spangled sky though the sprawling network of the old oaks' branches. She recognized a few familiar constellations, which warmed her just as it used to when she would lie on a blanket in the grass in front of her grandpa's small ranch house and stargaze. So many years and miles later, and she could see the same stars.

"Thank you, Bowen." She closed her eyes and spread out her arms and breathed in deeply. In on four. Hold four. Out on four. Hold four. Repeat. She wiggled her fingers, trying to catch the night. "I needed this."

She didn't know how long she stood here. She would have never guessed how peaceful Bowen was. He didn't fill in all the silent spaces with conversation. Without meaning to, she started swaying and humming one of her favorite Tom Waits's songs: "Hold On."

She made it through a verse and a chorus before she realized what she was doing and who she was doing it with. Her eyes snapped open. Bowen was watching her, a little curious, but no judgment clouded his expression.

"I used to wonder what the trees thought," she said, a little self-consciously. "Their arms stretched out so wide. What did they want to embrace?" Her mom had played games like that with her—maybe. Langston liked to pretend that she had at least. Her grandpa had once told her that her mom was a creative free spirit who couldn't be tamed. So Langston made up stories about what her mom had been like, how her mom had played with her and loved her, why she had to leave.

Bowen looked at the oak trees standing sentry around

them, protecting the courthouse, but Langston doubted he was fanciful.

"I wondered if the trees liked me. If they cheered me on when I raced. Laughed when I fell."

Would she please shut up? What was she trying to do, scare the man back to his truck? She'd developed a filter in college pretty quickly. She'd had to, and it had been easy because she'd been bucked so hard and so far out of her element, she hadn't felt like herself anymore.

And now, one week back in Marietta, one walk with a cowboy and her imagination and mouth kicked in.

She laughed to show him she was in on the joke that was herself and spun around to face the courthouse instead of the town she'd thought she'd left forever years ago.

Hold on. The melody played in her head. Wanted to come out. She closed her eyes against the burning prick of tears. Lord, she'd never been a crier. She was a fighter, but after the past few months, she hardly recognized herself.

Cowgirl up!

And then she realized Bowen was humming along. Deep, barely there. But his voice was so rich and dark, like espresso and dark chocolate poured over gravel, and it gave the song the poignancy it deserved. She felt something inside her crack open.

"That song is so beautifully constructed. The words. The melody. It's so hopeless, and yet there is still a tendril of hope," he said.

"Maybe that's all one needs—a tendril," she whispered.

One hot tear escaped and another. Langston dashed them away. Crying never solved a problem. Solutions were all on her. She'd grown up with those words ringing in her ears, a constant companion, reminding her to hone her will to fight and to win.

Hold on.

Maybe it was that simple. Two words to usher in the next phase of her life. Shoving aside the knowledge that she was alone with Bowen-frickin'-Ballantyne, she jumped into the moment and began to sing the second verse. He joined in, harmonizing, and then as if it were the most natural thing to do, one of his work-hewn arms slid around her body and he took one of her hands in his much larger one, urging her into a dreamy dance—just the two of them in the grass on the edge of Main Street with only the scattered oaks and empty courthouse windows as an audience. They alternated vocals but shared the chorus, and it was better than any date she'd ever had—including the theoretically romantic ones with Mason.

And this wasn't even a date. It was a walk. Bowen Ballantyne was that magic, that potent. Langston didn't immediately realize she'd closed her eyes or that they stopped dancing. She was so lost in the moment. Her childhood slipped away. The town's judgment and expectation and sympathy all drifted off. Even Mason's betrayal wasn't a blip on her radar. And the biggest loss was, for the moment, leashed and quiet.

"I always wondered what it would be like to dance with

no music playing."

"We made our own," he said.

She drew in his masculine grass, horse and earthy scent deep into her lungs and then looked up into his lean face. His expression in the moonlight filtering through the leafy branches was inscrutable.

"I'm right here," Bowen said, repeating a few words of the song. "What are you afraid of letting go?"

✪

NOSY WASN'T HIS style. Nosy meant connections. But Lang—Langston was Montana. Home. And she looked defeated. Not something he ever would have expected. And yet tonight he'd seen glimpses of the mouthy, daring, spirited girl he remembered. Hearing her talk about what trees thought and watching her sway and look so lost while she hummed, made him feel like he'd taken a hoof to his chest without his protective vest. And all because she'd been badly hurt.

Something unfamiliar stirred deep inside him. Woke up. He knew he was in trouble.

"I guess we're all holding on to something we shouldn't," he mused to cover for the fact she didn't answer.

"You more than most."

That was the trouble when you had a history with a woman—not necessarily a romantic one, but a history of time and place. Familiarity. Her grandpa and his had been good friends once, and just because you thought you knew someone, you could make assumptions. And assumptions could spin into a hella tangled Texas two-step.

"I finally got my dance." Her beautiful lips quirked.

"Pardon?"

"So polite, Bowen Ballantyne." She laughed, and he felt a flash of relief. There she was again. "You once promised you'd dance with me after the close of the teen summer rodeo circuit."

The spit dried in his mouth.

"I didn't."

"You did." He saw a hint of fire in her eyes, and her distractingly full, pouty lips twitched into a smile so sweet and so fleeting he already missed it.

"You were twelve."

"Thirteen—well, almost—and you were sixteen driving your granddad's truck, so full of yourself."

"That's probably true," he admitted. As the oldest he'd had a lot of firsts before his cousins.

"And I'd been afraid that no one would ask me to dance at the end of the rodeo party. Your granddad and mine promised me that you would ask me—I reminded you of your promise, but you never asked."

"A bribe or threat," Bowen mused. "Romantic."

She scoffed, "You're still not gallant."

"Never was. That's all Bodhi and Beck."

He recalled now that Beck had asked Dandelion to dance, and a few other ranch kids had harassed him until

Bodhi had threatened their jewels. And then Bodhi had danced with her.

Had he really been that much of an aloof idiot so worried about his cool factor?

"Well, thank you for the dance, fourteen years too late." She curtsied, grinning impishly.

That had not been a dance. He wasn't sure what it was. He still felt off-center, and the words that nearly jumped out of his mouth next made him grit his teeth. He would not ask her to the steak dinner and dance. He would not ask her to dance at the event. This was Marietta and their families had a history. Carol Bingley, the town gossip, and her Daughters of Montana would have them married by month's end. Although…even as the idea bloomed, he squelched it. No. And hell no. He was not lassoing Langston into Bodhi's game. A family rivalry born in the crib had to have limits.

"Let's keep walking," she said softly, the husky catch in her voice more pronounced than ever.

Her fingers brushed his, and he surprised himself by closing his hand briefly around hers. So small but mighty.

"You might have a job in a fancy hotel now," he said without thinking, "but you've still got the calluses of growing up ranch."

She pulled her hand away.

Dang. He'd just been thinking of what they had in common, but of course women wouldn't want to hear their hands felt rough.

This is why I let Bodhi or Beck do the talking.

"I didn't mean it like that," he admitted. He preferred women who worked with their hands and who were strong and who valued the land—that is, if he were looking for a woman, which he was most definitely not.

He inwardly cursed Bodhi again for planting the rodeo bride seed. Langston would be too believable. His granddad would buy the farce—hook, line, sinker. He'd have a preacher out to the house and a county clerk to issue the license the minute Bowen showed up with Langston at the ranch.

He'd hurt her again.

So definitely no.

"No more roping, wrestling or riding for me." Her voice sounded a little forced, as was her laugh. "Now I harness staff, wrestle guests, and rope in local businesses to plan and execute and ensure the magic happens, but yeah. I think I'd need a sand blaster to get my hands town-girl smooth."

"You must still ride."

He couldn't imagine Lang not on the back of a horse.

She stopped as they took their first step on the bridge that spanned the Marietta River and led to the fairgrounds the town had to rebuild after a fire a few years ago. He waited, curious but trying not to show it. If someone had once told him that he'd meet a grown-up Lang—the dandelion of Marietta, Montana—and she'd not be challenging him to a race on the back of a horse or running her mouth with a million opinions, he would not have believed them.

"No. Not anymore," she said, still standing in the dirt

path as if not willing to take that next step onto the bridge.

Dang. Could he do nothing right?

"Langston? We don't have to walk to the fairgrounds. I'm happy to walk you back to your car," he offered.

"No." She squared her shoulders. "Let's walk to the fairgrounds and then to the rodeo grounds. I've been thinking as we've been walking."

"Should I be scared?"

"More than likely. But you're tough."

"Coming from you, I'll take that as a compliment."

"Look at you, all charm and swagger." Langston took a deep breath. "I'm still not committed to the idea, but if you're lucky, cowboy, I might have a proposition that's a little more subtle than the one I made so many years ago."

"I find myself wanting to say yes."

Chapter Four

WHO WOULD HAVE thought the rodeo grounds that had hosted the Copper Mountain Rodeo for more than ninety years would be so evocative? But Langston paused at the entrance by a life-sized metal sculpture of a cowboy on a saddleless bucking bronc, hand high in the air. She squeezed her eyes shut and took a deep breath. Then she squared her shoulders and walked past the statue.

"So many memories here," he said neutrally. Good ones, he would have thought. From the time he'd been young he'd been fascinated by the rodeo and had wanted to compete. All of them had. And Langston had been a fierce competitor.

Why had she stopped?

They both walked side by side—she bumped him a few times, which he liked—past several of the outbuildings that housed various exhibits during the fair or the rodeo. They ended up stopping at one of the large livestock buildings. Massive fans were mounted in the ceiling, and the temporary corrals had already been set up and labeled for the registered animals. Sawdust had been laid down in the pens and mounds of it piled up at the ends of the building.

Langston breathed in deeply. "I do miss that smell," she

said, smiling.

"Even after the animals arrive?"

"It's even better then." She turned to look at him and flashed a smile—there and gone in a blink—that staggered him a little. "Smells like challenge and competition." She stared through the metal bars at the emptiness beyond.

"Why'd you give up competing?"

Her jaw tightened.

Dang, he just kept stepping in it with her. How did Bodhi navigate conversations with women so well and Bowen, who usually kept his mouth shut, couldn't ask the most basic of questions without messing up?

"A college degree was supposedly my ticket out," she said flatly.

"It's a useful thing to have," Bowen said, feeling his way. "My mom would have drop-kicked me from Denver to Nebraska if I'd backed down from my promise to get a degree before going pro."

"Tough cowgirls will do that."

"Don't ever let her hear you refer to her as a cowgirl." Bowen laughed. "She's a burr in my saddle." He had Lang's full attention, and he liked it. Her beautiful eyes shone. "She's a real estate agent who sells multimillion-dollar-plus properties. She has clients all over the world. Bad enough she had to grow up ranch, in her opinion. Coupled with a son and two nephews on the professional rodeo circuit, if she heard you refer to her as a cowgirl, her head would launch into orbit."

Langston laughed, and the lighthearted sound bounced off the metal building.

"She doesn't even own a pair of boots anymore except ski boots and boots with spiked heels that could take out a man's eye."

"Really?"

He nodded. "She wanted to leave the dirt and small town behind."

"I wanted to stay," Langston said softly.

"Why didn't you?"

"Nothing to stay for," she said. "Ranching's hard. My grandpa struggled to hold the ranch together for years, hoping my daddy would come home and stay, but he never did."

Bowen nodded. Ranching was hard. There were lean years and leaner. The Three Tree Ranch had been lucky to survive more than once.

"He had to sell off land to pay…well, to pay for, you know, my daddy's…" she waved her hand "…lifestyle and choices." Her voluptuous mouth—too wide for her pixie face—had an odd charm that held him like a spell even when she frowned. She looked so kissable.

Kiss Langston? Why did his mind go there? He made it a point to avoid local entanglements. Discipline was his religion.

"Let's go look at the arena." She strode off, her carriage straight, moves efficient like the cowgirl she'd once been.

Her father had been a bull rider who'd grabbed too

much life by the horns—whiskey, women, gambling. He won big and lost bigger. But, man, to see him on the back of a bull before his lifestyle bucked him off and kicked him hard had been a thing of beauty.

She climbed up to the top of the railing and settled facing the arena, the slim, straight line of her back strong and graceful. Was she remembering any of her or her daddy's rides?

"Your dad was my inspiration—well, for the bull riding."

She turned to face him. Her beautiful eyes glimmered with fire, and her delicate features looked almost mystical in the muted light, as if she were a rodeo fairy.

"Mine too," she said sadly. "When he was around it was like everything and everyone came alive. He was magic. He made me feel like I could do anything, be anyone. Charisma for miles."

"He told me once when I was ten and already fixing to be a professional cowboy that bull riding makes a man," Bowen said. "He said if you can stare down an eighteen-hundred-pound bull determined to have his say every day at work, you're not afraid of anything."

"Hopping on the back of a bull was the only thing he wasn't afraid of," Langston said. "And that's not my definition of a man." Her voice held an edge, and her eyes flinted while her jaw jutted. She looked so much like the little lionheart of his summers.

"A man sticks around and builds a life. He supports his family and keeps his promises." Langston's voice hardened even more.

Bowen felt like she'd thrown a punch. He'd never made a promise he didn't intend to keep, but while he'd admired her father as a bull rider, he supposed his long absences and hard living would have felt like indifference to the young girl left behind with a disappointed old man. Guilt slithered through Bowen. He'd always thought of her as a kid, a nuisance—quick to take offense, mouth off and seize a dare. She'd been volatile and alone, trying to prove herself in the arena with kids much older. And she'd navigated all of it without the loving support of family.

He'd always had his cousins and his granddad. His mom had made sure that he had what he needed: a safe, clean home; supplies; good education; nutrition.

"My dad left when I was eight," Bowen said, not sure why he told her, only that he felt like he owed her something—an attempt to connect. "He was a corporate attorney who traveled a lot and—" he hated admitting this "—took advantage of his time on the road. Within a year of the divorce, he'd remarried and had a baby on the way. I still saw him growing up, but not enough, and his new wife didn't like me much."

Now as an adult he understood better. He'd been angry, full of self-righteous blame. No wonder she hadn't wanted a resentful and sullen preteen and later teen around her new, growing family. In between his father's studied indifference, his stepmom's criticisms and his mother's cold bitterness, Bowen had shut all of them out, turning to his granddad and cousins for the sense of family and belonging.

"Did that sour you on the idea of marriage?" Her vibrant, whiskey-colored gaze bored into his.

Bowen sucked in a breath. Had it? He'd only thought of marriage in the abstract—something far down the road. Probably not for him. But maybe she had a point.

"I haven't seen a lot of happy marriages," he admitted. "My mom and Bodhi's mom all had marriage bust-ups that made them angry and bitter and definitely not willing to try again. Beck's mom took four swings before giving up." He looked away from her direct and luminous gaze toward the empty grandstands that would be teeming with families by Saturday. "Most of the marriages on the rodeo tour don't last."

"I don't even remember my parents together, but that didn't sour me," Langston said softly.

"That's good," he said, hearing the doubt in his voice.

What was wrong with him? What was wrong with all of them? Bodhi rarely resisted the urge to keep it in his pants. Beckett had had the same girl since high school, but fourteen years later still hadn't pulled the trigger on marriage. And him? The one-night hookups left him emptier and feeling dirtier than a bar at closing time but trying to build more seemed beyond his skill set.

Stick to what you're good at.

Marriage and kids just seemed like so much responsibility, and he already felt his back was about to break with the burdens of worrying about his granddad's health and whether the moms were manipulating him. The ranch. His mom's wild mood swings if she skipped her meds. Bodhi's increasingly reckless behavior, his aunts insisting he quit the rodeo tour so the cousins would too—only Bowen wasn't sure they would, which is why he stayed.

"This is not something a woman would normally tell a man," Langston said, her smile mischievous, "but since this is a walk, not a date, I can confess my big secret."

He found himself fighting back a smile. "Hit me with it, cowgirl."

She gulped in a breath, and her warm gaze collided with his. He could read a touch of embarrassment layered with sorrow, but he also saw courage there. Strength. Honesty.

"I wanted to get married," she said in a soft rush of words. "Even when I was young and in college. I wanted the whole thing. The boyfriend who was crazy about me. To get married after my college graduation. To have a husband. A house with the yard and a garden or a small ranch. A baby. Somewhere to belong. Someone to belong to. I wanted it all."

Her confession made him sad. She sounded ashamed, and a woman shouldn't feel ashamed for wanting to be loved and to build a life with a man. He couldn't ignore the ache in her voice or the reason behind it.

"Marriage success isn't great odds, worse for people whose folks divorced. I was sure I could beat the odds—even with my family history—sure if I wanted it enough, worked hard enough, I could have the family and the home I always wanted."

Her voice bounced off the metal of the building and rang into the night.

At least she'd had the guts to go after what she wanted.

He stood on life's sidelines, unwilling to make a commitment.

"Langston, the girl I grew up with during the summers had a will tougher than tanned cowhide. You want those things, you'll get them."

"This Friday was supposed to have been my wedding day," she said, flooring him. He hadn't known that fiery Langston Carr had been so deeply in love that she'd committed her heart and her life and her soul to a man's care. And then that man had let her down.

Like her daddy.

And her grandpa to some extent. Yes, he'd seen to her care and raised her, but the man Bowen knew hadn't seemed like a nurturing type. A ranch hand or parent of a friend often drove her to competitions. She often didn't have someone in the stands cheering her on, whereas he and his cousins had always had their granddad's presence and support.

"Langston, I'm sorry," he said inadequately, because it was obvious that she was not getting married on Friday. Her finger sported no ring or even a tan line to indicate that she'd recently been wearing a ring.

"I was going to get married at the Graff to a man I thought was the opposite of my daddy. Turns out he was the opposite in some ways, but not in the one that truly mattered."

Bowen didn't know what to say. Her eyes were dry as her gaze met his, but still he found himself wanting to comfort her. He covered her hand with his. Hers was so small. Cool in the mid-September night, but strong.

"Guy's an idiot to have lost you."

"A douche."

"A jerk."

"A donkey's ass."

"Twelve miles of bad road."

"Twenty."

Langston's laugh spilled out. "I'd forgotten we used to do that—try to one-up each other verbally."

Her whiskey eyes glimmered with warmth and humor and her shorn hair that hugged her head and emphasized her wide, lightly freckled cheeks glowed as if reflecting the moon. His hand still covered hers, and to Bowen's surprise, he didn't want to pull away.

"Which is funny, as you didn't talk all that much," she reminisced, "but sometimes you'd talk to me."

Who was being the douchey jerk now? Langston was likely grieving her lost dreams, and he was practically holding her hand, leaning into her on a moonlit night like an ambitious understudy.

Her hand fluttered under his, but instead of pulling away, she flipped her hand so that their palms connected, and their fingers interlaced.

A comfortable silence enveloped them, which Bowen rarely felt with anyone, and as he marveled at it, the significance of the words she'd said finally hit him.

"The Graff, this Friday?" he repeated. And Shauna, the inebriated woman he'd helped to her hotel room, had been her cousin, she'd said. So what was up with that?

As if he'd asked the question aloud, Lang's beautiful mouth tightened then twisted. Her pale eyebrows arched. "Same date. Same groom. Same venue. Different bride."

✪

"I DON'T KNOW what to say," Bowen finally said after she'd fake-laughed out her confession—to Bowen, of all people—the best-looking, most honest and reliable cowboy she'd ever come across. Of course he wouldn't know what to say. He likely couldn't fathom what her fiancé had done—easily, and not really with any remorse that she'd been able to twig.

She hopped off the fence into the arena. Heck, she'd rather face a distressed horse that had tossed her than Bowen right now, but here they were, and it wasn't in her nature to back down from a challenge. Hopefully, it never would be, and she dug deeper for courage to present him with the plan that had started to form in the Graff lobby.

"How about yes," she said, feeling reckless, and why not? It was dark. She was back in her hometown. Alone. Starting over. Again. Why act like her proverbial tail was between her legs? Go big or go home, right? Well, she was already home, so big it was.

"Pardon?"

Ever the cowboy. No *what* for Bowen Ballantyne. Her heart clenched. And she wanted to kick herself all over again for falling for Mason's city-raised charm, Ivy League education and bigger ambition fueled by family connections.

"Be my pretend boyfriend for the next few days leading up to the wedding."

"I'm not sure exactly what you are asking me to do," Bowen said, gracefully swinging down off the fence to land lightly beside her.

What was she thinking? Bowen was the most honorable man she knew. He wouldn't engage in subterfuge of any kind. She'd be better off asking Bodhi. He'd probably do it just for kicks. But he'd want something. And he'd probably take it to a level she was not prepared to go.

"Okay, just listen before you say no." She held her hand up. "And then instead of saying no, say yes."

"Lang—"

"Ston," she interrupted fiercely.

"You never cared before," he said, leaning back against the arena fence, one boot crossed over the other and his thumbs tucked above his brass-colored buckle in the unconsciously sexiest cowboy pose ever.

Really, what had she found appealing about Mason and his suits? Three years with him and a few minutes in a real cowboy's presence, and she was seriously having to remind herself not to jump him.

This will be pretend—if he even said yes.

"Here goes." She forced herself to stand in front of him and look him in the eyes, resisting crossing her arms defensively.

"I worked with Mason's mother, who owned an event planning business, the biggest one in the state. I met Mason while working some of the political fundraising events in Helena, and I've always been interested in politics, so we would talk and challenge each other's ideas. It was invigorating, and then we started dating."

Dang, Bowen listened with his whole body, and she was stalling. She could feel her breathing kick up and her throat tighten. She just needed to get through this part.

"Hey." And then Bowen was at her side, his thumb barely tracing the line of her cheek to her jaw. "Easy now." She might have been a spooked horse with how gentle he was. "You don't have to tell me anything, Langston, except what you need me to do."

The warmth and relief that washed through her scared her to death. She'd been on her own for so long. Even when she'd been with Mason, she'd never felt this level of caring, this solidarity of "I've got your back." She did with Bowen. That said so much about him and was all the warning she should need to not pitch this pathetic plan. But she had her pride.

And she wasn't a quitter.

"Long story short, we dated three years. When I—" She broke off as a wave of pain crashed through her. No. She couldn't and wouldn't go there. Maybe ever. "We decided to get married." Not exactly how it had played out, but close enough. "And…" She paused. There was so much else. The townhouse. The decorating. The dreams. "I helped my younger cousin, Sheila, Shauna's twin, get an internship at the company in the Missoula office during the summer before her last semester of college, and then Mason's mom hired her after she graduated, and a couple of months later I…I discovered Mason and Sheila together," she finished in a rush.

In the townhouse they'd purchased together but never lived in. In the bed she had bought for them to sleep in as they started their new life together.

"I broke off the engagement," she said woodenly looking away from Bowen's increasingly incredulous expression.

"He cheated on you with your cousin."

"And since the wedding was already planned and paid for by Mason's family, and they had a lot of family and rich, important and politically connected friends flying in and had rented quite a few area vacation estates and had so many Montana recreational activities planned…" She trailed off.

"You're saying your fiancé cheated on you with your cousin and is now marrying your cousin on your wedding day in the ceremony that you—as the bride—planned out." Bowen looked equally pissed and incredulous.

Langston nodded.

"Why the hell are you attending, cousin be damned?" he demanded.

"I'm not. Not as a guest anyway, but Mason's mom fired me after we broke off the engagement."

Because I'm "flawed goods."

Or a liar.

Take a pick.

"She fired you?"

"Please stop repeating everything. It's not helping."

Neither was the glare he leveled over her left shoulder or his tense posture.

"I have to be at the wedding because after Mason's mom fired me, I needed another job, and so I grabbed the first one I was offered, which happened to be at the Graff Hotel. It's temporary—a year. I'm filling in for an extended maternity leave. I never dreamed Mason and Shelia would marry so quickly and use the same venue, date or planned guest activities. Even the cake is the same type that Mason and I tasted and ordered. The only thing different is the bride and her dress."

He ran his hand through his hair and stared at her in total disbelief. It felt so good to see the same reaction in someone, an honest reaction, and to know that she wasn't crazy.

"Mason is going to make a run for state senate, and his family thought the optics of a small town would look good for his campaign videos as part of his biography." She made quotes around *optics*, and the noise Bowen made in the back of his throat was truly epic.

She looked out across the dirt arena. "Despite their

wealth, they are tight and always looking for an advantage." She toed the sawdust on the arena floor. "I made excuses for their behavior because I so desperately wanted to be a part of a big family. I wanted to belong, and with his family and the job and the connections I felt…safe—like I had a home and a life that wouldn't disappear."

Langston was sure she couldn't sound needier or more desperate. Bowen took a step toward her then stopped short.

"They couldn't really have kept all the reservations the same just to not lose a deposit," he growled.

"I'm sure that figured in, but also, Mason's campaign launch is part of it. When I was planning the events, I was told to think of authentic Montana and its history as I booked activities, and to think of the visuals."

"Because good TV visuals and disrespecting a woman you pledged to love and protect is authentic Montana," he sneered.

Langston stared at him. "No one's ever stood up for me," she marveled, not censoring her thoughts. "No one I knew—my so-called friends and my colleagues said they were sorry that I lost the…Mason and the townhouse and my job."

Her whole life.

No one had helped. Instead, she'd felt like people avoided her as if she had a contagious disease.

Bowen didn't move. And his gritted jaw looked like Walt Longmire's on a bad day. He was so devastatingly sexy when he shouldn't have been. She should be done with men for at least a couple of years, right? When was her sense of self-preservation going to kick in?

"Say something," she prompted.

"What do you want me to do? Take him behind the arena and bust his jaw?"

It was so Marietta. But not Bowen, at least she didn't think so.

"Tempting, but his family's very connected and he'd have you up on assault charges."

"If they found the body."

She laughed. "I was thinking maybe something less violent."

"I wasn't."

And just those two words, or maybe it was his reaction to the story—half of which, the worst of which, he didn't know—cracked something open inside her, letting in a shaft of light. She felt less alone. And for the first time in three months, she felt like yes, she was in pain, and she'd made a horrible mistake, but she would be okay and eventually she would find happiness.

"And think how colorful the purple, red and yellow bruises on his face would look on TV."

Langston didn't bother holding back her smile.

"So what do you want me to do?"

"Well, it's, um, embarrassing to ask."

Epic understatement.

"A bit more like our show in the lobby?"

She blushed even as relief flooded her that she didn't have to say the ask out loud.

"A little more PG than G?" he asked. "A guy's gotta get prepared."

Had Bowen always been so tall—wide shoulders, rangy body that was so tightly muscled? And his face was as hard-hewn as Copper Mountain. How was he still single? She so shouldn't be asking herself that question. She didn't want to date him. Not for real. She definitely wasn't ready to date again. And she'd never be prepared for a man like Bowen. What had she been thinking at sixteen? She'd been more courage than sense.

Stay in your lane, as Mason's mom often said to her.

"Come on, Dandelion," he said. "Not like you to zip it. What do you need? Spill."

She huffed out a breath.

"This would be easier if you weren't standing there looking so…so…hot!" She clapped her hand over her mouth. "I just said that," she mumbled.

"That you did," he admitted, grinning at her uncool lunacy.

"I blame being back in Marietta," she said. "Let's walk. This will be easier if I'm not looking at you."

"My hotness burning up your corneas all the way to your brain?"

She shot him a quick look and then hopped over the arena fence so that she could head toward the Marietta River. Running water always soothed her.

"Stick to the bulls. You're not that funny," she muttered. "Is Bodhi missing his sense of humor? Or have you been holding out on all of us?"

"Still waters run deep." He fell into step with her. "Or they drown you."

Langston felt like she was drowning.

"Stop running, Lang, we're not kids anymore. Spit it out. You're worrying me that I really will have to hide a body."

Yah, she was running away. She needed to stop.

She paused by the low bank of the river. By mid-September, the river resembled more of a cheerful but lazy creek after the heat of the short, dry summer.

"I want to show Mason and his family and my cousins that I'm okay with…with everything."

"Why would you be?" Bowen was outraged.

"You have your pride," she said stiffly as he opened his mouth again. "I have mine."

He pressed his lips together as if to keep from interrupting or objecting. Langston marveled, remembering all the times Mason had interrupted her when she'd been sharing a story about her day or adding her opinion of something he'd been talking about.

"What Sheila did was wrong. And Mason betrayed me. They both betrayed me. There's more to the story, but I don't want to go into that now. The point I want to make to them is that I've moved on. I'm fine." She swallowed hard, determined to ignore the feeling of unease that snaked through her. It felt like a warning.

"But you're not fine," Bowen said softly.

"I will be."

"I know, Dandy. I know." His hand cupped the back of her head briefly.

"The way they treated me and what they are doing now hurts, but I do think I dodged a bullet with Mason and his family. A man who could do that after—" She broke off. "And with my cousin while he and I were planning our wedding and in our marriage bed is not a good man."

"Agreed."

"So I was hoping that you could…you know, um…visit me a few strategic times at work and around town and act friendly."

"Friendly?"

Why was she still so hella awkward?

"How friendly?"

Was he deliberately being obtuse?

"Dating. I'd like you to pretend that we are dating."

"Casually?"

She balled her hands at her sides to stop the shaking and went for broke. "Fine. Since you want it spelled out, I'd like you to pretend that you are crazy head over boots in love and lust with me, Bowen Ballantyne, until the wedding, which is Friday midmorning."

She wasn't sure what she expected, but the smile that slowly dawned, and the wicked heat and amusement in his eyes lit a fire inside her, and Langston felt like she'd taken more than one step too far toward the edge.

CHAPTER FIVE

THE NEXT MORNING, with the sun still not clearing the Absaroka Range, Bowen parked his truck on Main Street and strode toward the Graff Hotel to meet Langston for breakfast. He felt hungover without the benefit of the alcohol buzz of fun the night before. The trip home and the Copper Mountain Rodeo was always one of the highlights of his year. But this week was heading into all kinds of awful—first his granddad's bombshell about possibly selling the ranch, then the moms all visiting, likely to railroad Granddad into a commitment. Bodhi's insane game and now Langston needing a favor.

Bodhi would say his stars were aligning.

Bowen doubted that.

Helping Langston out and roping her into his game would go two ways to sideways before it blew up in both of their faces.

Big Bang Theory, cowboy style.

Sure, he could help her out. Hardly a chore to be attentive and squire around a beautiful, funny and fiery woman, and it could play right into Bodhi's playful scheming. But using Lang that way was all kinds of wrong. She'd already been hurt. He'd help her out. And help Granddad and best Bodhi and Beck in a different way—somehow.

A favor for a favor sounded easy, but Bowen's life didn't roll like that.

Bowen ran up the wide circular staircase of the Graff and pulled open the door to the lobby. He spotted Lang across the room wearing another power suit. This one was a maroon pantsuit that clung to her slim, athletic curves. Bowen blinked trying to reconcile the image of Lang as a young teen, the wounded but still determined woman last night wearing sexy jeans and now the corporate version.

Fascinating.

Maybe he should have texted and waited in his truck, but she said she wanted him in the lobby. He waited, feeling all kinds of stupid. Langston finished talking, tucked her tablet back into a small messenger-style cross-body bag and looked up. Her whiskey gaze clashed with his, and he felt thirsty.

Was anyone watching that she wanted to watch?

Bowen realized he didn't know his role yet.

Might as well practice. He'd seen Bodhi walk across a room, his eyes targeted on a woman while the woman melted under his laser focus enough times he should be able to not make an utter fool of himself.

The sun shafted through one of the lobby windows, spotlighting her. And that was as good a sign as any. Bowen held his Stetson by the crown and advanced across the lobby floor, gaze honed on Lang, and everyone and everything else just faded away.

OH. MY. GOD.

Bowen Ballantyne was walking toward her, and his walk was the most devastatingly hot and fluid thing Langston had ever seen. The spit dried in her mouth and as he came closer, she waited to burst into flames. When a sunbeam slanted through the window lighting up them both, she nearly slapped her arms and legs thinking that she'd spontaneously combusted.

He looked good enough to eat. Devour, if she were honest. Worn Wranglers that hugged his lean, muscular thighs, hung a bit low on his hips. A belt buckle testifying to another win. And a light blue western-style shirt open at his tan throat, his sleeves rolled up.

Lust rose fast, hot and intense, and raced through her. No surprise. Bowen had always been her ideal man for more years than she wanted to admit. She'd thought she'd managed to shelve the attraction. And for the past few months she'd felt dead inside.

She welcomed feeling alive again, but she kicked her heart a bit. Bowen was doing her a favor. That was all. Then he was heading right back out of town and on the road. She would be too after the Graff gig. She'd beef up her résumé, make as many connections as she could—hopefully, Mason's mom wouldn't blackball her. There was no reason for that. She hadn't fussed or fought or gone to the press.

Then Bowen was here, taking her hands she'd been fisting up near her chest like an idiot, virginal miss in a spaghetti western in his warm ones. He leaned in close to her. Her nervous musings quieted, and her world narrowed down to Bowen.

Too close. She could smell him—pine, grass, leather and all masculine heat. She breathed him in, suddenly starving. His gray-blue eyes, set off spectacularly by the shirt, darkened as they searched hers, and his pupils flared, as did his nostrils.

"Hi," she whispered breathily.

Jeez! She'd had more flirty, go-out-and-get-what-you-want skills when she'd been thirteen and decided that Bowen Ballantyne was the hottest boy in Montana, competition over, winner declared, trophy awarded.

"Good morning," he rumbled.

One hand covered both of hers. Warm and strong and comforting even as her pulse skyrocketed. This close, she could see that he had darker specks in his irises and thick lashes that had a hint of curl, as if God had thought his face was too hard, masculine perfection, and he needed an angel kiss of something feminine.

Was he going to kiss her?

Her tips tingled, softened, as if answering his unspoken question.

Yes, please.

Bowen Ballantyne had made his feelings clear years ago, and it wasn't as if the intervening years had been particularly kind or had added an irresistible sexy, feminine sparkle to her.

His gaze dipped to her lips and then back to her eyes. The heat inside of her built and flowed, making her limbs feel liquid.

"Mornin', to you too, cowboy." She tried to ease the sexual tension rocketing up inside of her. They were supposed to be pretending, and this was feeling too real, too quickly.

She'd made a serious miscalculation.

"Ma'am," he shot back.

She couldn't choke back the dumb girl giggle, and Bowen's sensuous, but rather stern mouth eased into the hint of a smile.

And then his lips covered hers, and she breathed him in going on instinct, whispering his name and kissing him back, hungry.

She had to stand on tiptoe to reach him, and her hands that had been pressed against her chest were now flattened on his pecs first before sliding up to grip his shoulders. Bowen's broad hand cupped the side of her face, and his forehead rested against hers. Their breath mingled.

"Are we going with the PG rating with a hint of R every now and then?" Bowen smiled.

"What?" Langston gulped in air. Her heart slammed in her chest.

The favor! She was so stupid. For Bowen, it was showtime.

Pull yourself together.

"When you're finished with the rodeo, Hollywood is holding a spot in a movie or two or three for you."

"Is that so?" His breath teased her lips, and without thinking, Langston kissed him again, falling into the heat of his mouth, the power of his kiss and the strength of his body.

Bowen slowly pulled away, still holding one of her hands. The other was gripping his shirt and snaps like she was going to get to all that hot, tanned goodness beneath.

"Easy, cowgirl." His low voice barely rumbled above a whisper. "We can't let the horse out of the barn yet."

Heat scorched her cheeks.

"I thought you wanted to start a couple of rumors, not get us arrested," he murmured.

She watched his lips move. She'd always loved his mouth. Well, the whole package that was Bowen Ballantyne, but his mouth had always fascinated her because he'd hid his thoughts and feelings so well even as a teen, and she thought his mouth might reveal a clue to what was going on inside his head.

"You know me, never subtle." She managed to engage her brain.

"True." He grinned, and her heart flipped over. She hadn't seen a playful Bowen. Even more captivating than a brooding Bowen.

"Can I take you to breakfast?"

"Yes. Main Street Diner is calling my name," she chirped. Hopefully, she could perky her way out of the hole of lust she'd just drilled halfway to China or Australia or whatever was on the other side of the globe from Montana. "And we can make a plan."

She was going to need one. Big-time. A plan for her to keep her hands and her heart and her imagination to herself. Rules to follow.

She and Bowen walked toward the exit, and Langston took a casual look around. It was early, but her aunt and a couple of her friends were watching her. Judith, her almost-future-mother-in-law, was filling up a traveler's coffee mug to take with her on her speed walk while she made her phone calls. She'd seen the kiss too.

"Mission launched," she whispered, feeling like she probably should immediately abort any mission involving romantic pretense with Bowen Ballantyne.

"Having fun?" he asked softly.

She was about to say something sarcastic, when she paused, and missed a step. Bowen easily kept her moving, no stumbling with this cowboy.

"Yes," she said, the reality of it hitting home. She looked up into his lean, angular face, his blue-gray eyes that missed nothing.

"I shouldn't be, but I am, just a little."

"Then I'm not doing a good job," Bowen said as he opened the door. They stepped out into a beautiful September morning. "I need to up your fun factor."

✪

"WHAT'S NEXT?" HE asked outside the hotel.

"You think I have a checklist?" she asked him haughtily. He tried to behave himself and not notice how the pantsuit highlighted her rounded ass in the conservative, slightly stretchy slacks. How were men supposed to concentrate when this was corporate attire? No wonder women were bossing up and showing men how it was done in so many professional fields. Damn biology.

Bowen tried not to notice how the cut of the maroon blazer emphasized her small waist that he was tempted to slide his arm around. They were pretend dating; would that be out of bounds? And then the flare from her waist showcased her hips.

Underneath the jacket, he could see a lacy orange blouse or tank that peeked through the deep V of the jacket.

It was driving him crazy. Or his dick was. It didn't care that this was pretend. It was all in.

"Do we hold hands?" he asked wanting to rile her up and distract his southern hemisphere from taking too much notice of unfolding events.

"Huh? Are there rules?"

"There should be," he said. "Ground rules."

"You're probably right. Are you a hand holder?"

His relationships had all been very transactional—on the road, dinner or drinks, maybe some dancing, and then sex.

One night. Or maybe a weekend at most. Not something he wanted to brag to Lang about.

"Let's see." He laced his fingers with hers, curious to see what she'd do or say.

They started walking down the curved stairs of the hotel.

"Hey!" Beck suddenly appeared. He'd stopped his truck in the middle of Main Street and stared. Looked pissed, and Bowen's morning got a bit brighter. Beck was alone and heading back in the direction of the ranch. Clearly, his morning scone and chai run to Ashni had not gone as well as Beck had hoped when he'd announced his plan back at the ranch.

He held Lang's hand as they crossed to Beck's truck.

"You remember Langston Carr, Beck?"

The shock on Beck's face was priceless. Damn. He should have captured that with his phone. Bodhi would have bought drinks, laughing, for the next month.

Beck looked stunned as he greeted her, clearly thinking Bowen had roped Lang into the game.

Good, let him sweat. But he didn't want to give Beck a chance to fire off any questions.

He slapped his hand on Beck's truck. "I'll see you back at the ranch." They had a long list of chores to accomplish both for the party and for the ranch. And that was before the moms showed up with the schemes they'd dreamed up. And now he'd committed to be a fake boyfriend for Langston.

A favor for a favor?

He pushed the thought away just as he had last night. He

needed to get Granddad alone. Get him to talk. Figure out what was really wrong and leave Langston out of it. She had enough troubles, and if he could help ease her back into single life and her hometown with her pride and head held high, he'd do it. She was local. He owed her for saddling her with that ridiculous nickname.

✪

FORTY MINUTES LATER, Bowen's stomach was happily full, but the rest of him was not.

"I intended to pay for breakfast," he said, likely for the tenth time.

Lang smiled sunnily. "Deal. It's the twenty-first century, and we were discussing business. You're doing me a favor."

"That makes me feel like a gigolo."

She laughed, which did not help his mood.

"Is that even a thing? Has no hot babe ever paid for your breakfast?"

He didn't have to think about that one.

"Old-fashioned," she stated. "You can take me to dinner at Rocco's. And buy a bottle of wine." She definitely seemed happier now that they had a glimmer of a plan.

"I know you will be busy at the ranch, but in the evenings there will be members of the wedding party and prestigious guests around," Lang said thoughtfully. "Maybe late-night appetizers in the bar one night. You can pay for that and cocktails, see." She tapped her head. "I got a strategy for wooing, being seen and getting you to pick up the spendier tabs."

It was on the tip of his tongue to ask if they were only going to see each other where they might be seen, but luckily he zipped it. He wasn't really courting her.

He swallowed the bitterness that had lodged in this throat since last night. "Would you like me to walk you into your office?" he offered.

"Through the lobby. Is that okay?"

"Yeah."

He felt dumb and awkward.

"It feels strange, pretending," he admitted as they came to the top of the stairs and a valet swung open the ornate door for them. "I'm acting as I normally would, and yet it feels…" *Wrong* was what he wanted to say, but that seemed unfair.

"Changing your mind, cowboy?"

She tilted her head and her angular jaw jutted. It was a move he'd seen her make a lot as a kid, and it both charmed and reassured him. And when he saw the hint of vulnerability flash through her emotive eyes, something else woke deep inside him.

"Nope."

The relief in her expression filled him with conflicting feelings.

"You, lady, are dangerous," he said as they walked through the front door together, his palm at the small of her back. "It's been only about twelve hours since I've seen you after twelve or more years, and you're getting me all tied up into knots."

It was true. He didn't know if he was coming or going, and he probably should have kept his mouth shut because he wasn't sure who was talking—him or the pretend courting Bowen.

Not courting, idiot. Dating.

Courting was old-fashioned and implied specific and more permanent intentions.

She turned to face him, her body brushing his. Her thumb traced his lower lip.

"Checking for crumbs from the coffee cake you would not share." She licked the pad of her thumb, and Bowen felt as if she'd lit a stick of dynamite. "And don't worry about the knots. You remember how good I am with roping."

"Forgot I roped me a real cowgirl." He laughed—the sound bounced off the hard surfaces of the grand lobby. Usually Bowen aimed to be unobtrusive—head down, doing his job. Trying to be noticed, channeling his inner Bodhi, made him inwardly squirm.

"It's been a while since I roped me anything big." Her eyes glimmered through her mascaraed eyelashes that were long and curled dramatically. "I might need a little practice." She walked her fingers up the snap on his shirt.

"I've always got ropes in my truck." He caught her fingers. If they kept this up, he was going to have to adjust himself. He'd had more control in college.

"So, will I see you later tonight?" Langston asked.

"Yes."

"The perfect word from the perfect boyfriend." Lang sighed dreamily, her eyes glinting.

It was good to see her smile. He didn't often say things that amused women. It felt good to have a history with someone. Common ground.

He was aware of people in the lobby—sitting in a grouping of chairs, at the front desk checking in and out, in the bar eating breakfast and downing what looked like mimosas.

"I'll text." He settled on that. The ranch—unlike others in the area—had great cell reception. "I'm working the ranch this week and next, and you've got an…event to pull off."

"And others to plan. Lots of meetings this week, but I intend to watch you win All-Around Cowboy this year," she said flirtily, standing on tiptoes again to kiss him.

His heart flipped in his chest, and he tucked one finger under her chin.

He was liking this pretending a little too much.

"Dandelion! Girl, you've got that all wrong. This has-been's going to be gulping dirt this weekend, so your starry-eyed gaze will be glued to me as I win All-Around Cowboy."

"Bodhi Ballantyne." Langston peeled herself off of Bowen and turned around to face his grinning cousin, who had his arm around the statuesque auburn-haired beauty Bowen had seen him chatting up at Grey's last night. "You call me that dang childhood nickname one more time and you'll be eating through a straw. My daddy didn't teach me much but how to hit and how to ride, and I've kept in practice."

"Damn, girl." Bodhi laughed. "Simmer down." He turned to the woman, who looked to be wearing one of Bodhi's shirts belted with one of his belts and buckles and a fine pair of jeans that hugged her long legs.

Bowen stared. He wasn't surprised that Bodhi had hooked up with the woman. He did it nearly every weekend. But letting her wear a buckle was not only new, it was unbelievable. Bodhi cherished his buckles. Shined them. Stored them in a specially made box Beck had built for each of them during one of their tour breaks the first year he competed.

Bowen stared at the buckle. Maybe it wasn't what it appeared to be.

"Eyes up, cuz," Bodhi said, and while he still smiled, his eyes had gone navy blue and his tone got low like he was warning him off.

What?

Bowen had been staring at the woman rather intently and not at her face. But if he explained he was trying to figure out the mystery and the significance of the buckle, he'd sound deranged.

"Told you we breed 'em cowgirl tough in Montana," Bodhi said to his date. "You remember my cousin, Bowen Ballantyne," Bodhi said, all charm and good manners. "And Langston Carr, who grew up ranch on the Carr & Sons Ranch east of our place. We spent summers together on the youth and teen rodeo circuit. Best barrel racer I ever saw 'til I went pro."

What should have been a compliment made Langston stiffen like she'd been slapped. She even took a step back into his body. Bowen slid his hand around her waist instinctively.

"I'd love to see that. I haven't been to a rodeo, but I'm going this weekend." The woman ignored the sudden tension and smiled and reached out a hand. "Nico Steel," she said, and tossed her long, thick ponytail over her shoulder. "I'm on an impulsive vacation and stopped for a drink last night to figure out what to do with a week or two of unplanned time. Then I met Bodhi."

"He's good with a quick answer on how to spend time," Bowen said.

He didn't mean it to sound so mean. What in the hell was wrong with him?

"Nice to meet you, Nico." Langston shook her hand and introduced herself, and explained that she worked at the Graff. Nico was a guest.

"Sooooo." Nico drew out the word; her smile faltered. "The hotel just texted that I can have my room through the weekend," she said. "I know you'll be busy with the rodeo…"

"Not that busy." Bodhi smiled at her. "I'll text you later today." He leaned in and lightly kissed her. A light pink blush stained her cheeks. "My cousins and I work the ranch when we're here. And we've got our moms coming in a couple of days planning to ride our asses with more chores, but it's not all work and no fun." He played with her thick ponytail. "I can pick you up and bring you out to the ranch—maybe a picnic dinner and a horse ride?"

"That sounds amazing. Like something out of a brochure."

"I can personalize your tour far better than some brochure," he whispered in her ear but loudly enough for Bowen to hear.

"Perhaps you'd both like to join us," Nico invited, startling Bowen to his toes.

"Oh." Langston stared, deer in the headlights.

"Ummmm." He was even less quick on his feet.

"Girl, let's leave the inarticulate duo alone to find their own adventures," Bodhi said. "I want to keep you to myself for a while longer."

"But I thought—" He kissed her midsentence, stemming the flow of words. Then he took his hat he was holding—his favorite gray Stetson—and set it on her head.

"The sun's still hot enough to burn," he said one finger stroking her cheek. "So wear this when you go shopping or exploring today until you can buy your own. I'll see you later this afternoon or early evening—save that for me."

"Okay. Sounds good." She brushed his fingers with hers. "Nice to meet you, Bowen and Langston. Hope to see you both again soon."

She turned and ran up the wide staircase, her long legs making short work of the expansive stairs.

Bodhi watched her the entire time.

"Later, lovebirds." Bodhi smirked and strode back across the lobby. He even whistled, the bastard.

"What was that?" Langston breathed. "He just loaned a hookup his hat and a buckle from Deadwood." She turned to him. "And put his hat on her head. Does he have a head injury?"

"Dropped at birth and tossed off a lot of broncs and bulls."

"He's up to something. What is it?"

It was on the tip of his tongue to tell Langston about the Rodeo Bride Game, but this wasn't the place or the time. He wasn't sure there ever would be one. He wasn't sure what to do. Warn Nico? Kick Bodhi? Enlist Langston's help? She definitely had always been a fierce competitor. Or could he sit his granddad down and get him to spill?

Why did the best option pop up last on his radar?

"I have to go to work, Bowen," Langston reminded him as he struggled to figure out what to do. "Can we talk later today? Make a plan for tonight since you're still game."

He watched the door swing shut after Bodhi. Every woman in the lobby had marked his cousin's rolling, sex-on-a-stick walk across the restored hardwood floor.

"Oh, I'm definitely game," he told her. "For whatever you've got in mind."

Clearly, Bodhi was all in in a way that made the hair on the back of his neck prickle. And Beck was lost without Ash. And Granddad, his North Star was dark. Silent. And it was up to him to save them all.

✪

"WHAT THE HELL was that?" Bowen caught up with Bodhi outside the Graff. The valet was just handing Bodhi his keys.

"What the hell was that?" Bodhi tossed the question back in his face.

The valet was a young man—a boy, really—Joseph, Bowen read on his nametag.

"Thanks, man." Bodhi handed the kid a twenty and shooed him off with a quick wave of his hand.

"You're not really going through with your stupid challenge, are you?" Bowen demanded the minute the kid was out of earshot. "With Nico?"

"Stupid, is it?" Bodhi laughed, but his eyes flinted. "Meanwhile, Mr. Cowboy Never Do Anyone Local, is all but letting Langston Carr mount you like a horse about to compete in the rodeo in a hotel lobby where half the town is sure to see or hear about it. Don't play outraged gentleman cowboy with me."

Bodhi swung open the door of his truck.

"What are you doing, Bodhi, really?" Bowen grabbed the door. Bodhi had an edge to him lately. Bowen had felt it all year—his cousin teetering on a knife-edge, and he was going to cut himself real deep. "You don't want to hurt that girl."

"Woman. Who says I'm going to hurt her? Nico knows the score. I scratch her back, she scratches mine."

"Scratch. Is that the euphemism for what I think it is?"

"At least I'm up-front. I'm honest."

"Honest?" Bowen exploded. "What does that even mean to you? You pick up women like candy, and even though you say you're just passing through or whatever line you use, you know some of them hear something different. You know some of them are thinking that they're special, that you're going to want to stay."

Bodhi swung himself into his truck and jammed on his aviator-style sunglasses.

"I tell them the only thing I stick are bulls and broncs. I don't choose women who want more. Dandelion always had it bad for you, and you barely noticed she was alive."

That struck Bowen hard in his solar plexus. "You think you're the hero of this story?"

"Why not? Beck's fucked up with Ashni. She's finally had enough of his indecision. You're too much of a gentleman to tell Lang what we got going on."

"We don't have anything going on," Bowen nearly roared in frustration.

"You know you want to beat me, Bowen. You always want to beat me. You and Beck both. Take your best shot." He opened his arms. "It's all on the line. You really going to walk away and not play?"

"What is wrong with you?" Bowen felt like he'd run a mile under four minutes. Bodhi was out of control. He was going to get hurt.

"Nothing wrong." Bodhi grinned and jammed his keys into the ignition. "I'm winning. Can't win if you don't play,

Bow. You taught me that." Bodhi sped out of the parking lot and Bowen watched him disappear.

How could Bodhi make a game out of something so important? Pretending wasn't in Bowen's moral skill set. He wasn't good at it and didn't want to be.

But without his granddad, without the ranch, without the rodeo, without the cousins, Bowen didn't know who he'd be anymore.

Chapter Six

"WHAT THE HECK was that?" Shauna demanded, joining Langston from an overflow table at the bar where she'd been nursing a latte and, from the looks of it, a headache.

"Oh. Hey," Langston said coolly. "How are you feeling this morning?"

"Crap, but I wasn't drunk enough to forget that I brought that cowboy back to my room. You didn't."

Langston swallowed her quick retort. Shauna had moved away from Marietta as a young teen and had lived in Seattle since college and she was family, but for this week, she was part of the bridal party, so she was a job. A career. And after being fired by her would-be mother-in-law on no grounds that would hold up legally or that Langston could have controlled, she was going to need the recommendation from the Graff more than ever.

"He brought you back to the hotel lobby, Shauna. I took it from there." Langston smiled far more cheerily than she felt. "I tucked you in, got you aspirin, and an herbal-doctored glass of water guaranteed to kick a hangover to the curb."

"If I'd drunk all of it instead of argued with you like I always do," Shauna mumbled. "So you're saying I didn't...he and I didn't..." Shauna trailed off.

"No. Definitely not."

Shauna looked irritated. Lang was over the moon that Bowen was a gentleman.

It doesn't matter who he picks up or doesn't.

"My goal was to hook up with a cowboy, and you are saying that I didn't?"

"Nope. He was a total gentleman."

"But he is single?" Shauna asked speculatively watching the ornate lobby door swing shut behind Bowen.

"No." Langston, wondering if she'd have to be more adamant than that. "Bowen and I competed as teens in summer rodeo, and while I'm in town this year we're seeing where things go."

She said it so matter-of-factly. She could act! She could fake a relationship with Bowen and remain heart-whole while he sauntered off to the next city on the tour.

Shauna pouted for a moment, and then she touched Langston's arm. "I'm happy for you," she said. "Pissed that you snagged the hottest cowboy I've seen so far in town, but happy that you aren't dwelling on Mason too much."

"I'm not," Langston said truthfully. There had been too many hurts and lost dreams to focus on just the one he represented, and one walk with Bowen had made her wonder what she'd seen in Mason other than the family she'd craved. She pasted on her professional smile, not liking the turn of her thoughts. Bowen had a family, and Ben Ballantyne was a wonderful man.

"And you don't need to worry about one cowboy slipping your lead, come Thursday," Langston said, her heart happy that she'd get a chance to see Bowen a few times this week. "You will be up to your…" She broke off as Shauna laughed and cupped her breasts.

"Nipples in cowboys? I can live with that."

There were worse things in life.

"You should bring him to the wedding," Shauna suggested.

"No!" She was not over Mason enough to watch him pledge eternal love and devotion to her now pregnant cousin.

"But you're also family, Langston. Even if we don't see each other all that much, and it will make Sheila feel better that you've forgiven her."

Making Sheila feel better wasn't not on her agenda.

"Water under the bridge and all that," Shauna said airily, because she had not lost her fiancé, the family, the new home, her job and the future she'd thought she'd have.

Langston's face felt brittle as she tried to maintain a professional, I'm in control smile. Water under the bridge? Her cousin had known Mason Keen was her fiancé. She'd wanted him because he was rich and connected, and she thought he would make her life easier. Langston also knew for a fact that Sheila of the oh-so-sensitive heart had lied about being on birth control.

The irony made Langston want to slap someone. But she

was an event planner, not an event or life destroyer, so sucking it up, while not a natural part of her personality, had become an acquired professional skill set.

Maybe she needed to consider a new career after this year.

"I'll be busy making sure the wedding is a beautiful, memorable event," Langston said, sweetness and light. "But maybe at the end of the brunch after the cake cutting and bouquet toss, Bowen will join me for a dance among the flowers in the garden." She sighed dreamily as if picturing it, although she wasn't. The last thing she wanted to see was Sheila, with her barely there baby bump clinging to Mason and gazing at him like he was the second coming.

But on second thought, being held in Bowen's strong arms and gazing into his eyes while a local country band played would slay any doubts that she was still brokenhearted and crushed.

Bowen was hot. He was Montana cowboy hot—everything Mason wanted to be but wasn't. And she'd never met a cowboy who didn't know how to sweep a girl off her feet or move her around a dance floor. Bowen would be a far smoother, way sexier dancer than Mason on the best day in his imagination.

"Maybe I will," Langston mused, feeling a little mean, thinking of all the pretend cowboys on the guest list. She'd cleared the field for the treacherous Sheila and the cheating Mason, but it didn't mean she had to go quietly, head down into the night.

Langston bit back a laugh at the thought of the visual—she knew where the camera crews would be so she could make sure they got in the wedding and the campaign videos—at least before editing so that Mason's control-everything mom would see her happy and gazing into another man's eyes, a man who screamed Montana-born cowboy.

As the Ballantyne boys would say—rubbing their hands together, their various shades of blue eyes sparkling—game on!

✪

BOWEN REVIEWED THE list of chores with his granddad—not at the farmhouse-style kitchen table where they had made and adjusted the list and assigned chores since before the three grandsons had been nearing their teens, but instead they met up on Plum Hill—so named by Beckett when they'd been kids, because of the ten-plus wild plum trees that grew and produced even though their granddad didn't do anything to take care of them.

Ben Ballantyne was eating a late plum when Bowen drove up, the bed of his truck full of supplies.

His granddad tossed him a plum, and Bowen tossed him back a pastry bag. He'd gone to the Java Café to grab a few of his granddad's favorites.

Then he'd gone to Big Z's Hardware store to pick up the order for his granddad—paying off the rather large tab he'd run up, which made Bowen wonder again if his granddad was having cash flow issues. He might feel he had no recourse but to sell. Bowen's stomach cramped remembering how Langston's grandpa had sold pieces of his ranch over the years. He'd overheard him telling Granddad that it was like ripping out and selling pieces of his soul. But how to ask him about money without causing offense? Bowen didn't think even Bodhi could pull that off.

Lumber, white paint and cleaning supplies had made up the bulk of the order. "Looks like I'm up on the barn roof today," he greeted and pulled out the tool kit he always carried in his truck's lock box.

"Looks like." Ben Ballantyne peered into the bag. "This is a good trade for a plum." He laughed. "Cinnamon rolls are my favorite. Ashni makes a big tray of them every time she comes." Ben paused, and his still-clear, sharp blue gaze hardened as if Ashni and Beck having issues was his fault. "She's staying in town this time, but she promised me that she will come and make some of my favorites. Don't think I'll share with that fool Beckett."

Bowen bit into a plum. He didn't want to give himself time to think.

"So, paint." Bowen ignored the unspoken Beck relationship question. Not his area of expertise. He'd had a girlfriend in college for maybe half a year, but she'd dumped him because he spent too much time studying and being away competing. And then during his breaks he'd head home to Montana. He'd felt more relieved than brokenhearted. His experience had been casual and fleeting ever since.

Bowen looked at the barn and, next to it, an equipment shed. The barn was mostly used for feed and supply storage now, but because of the view and the access to a ranch road and the electricity, each year it was shined up for the annual Ballantyne Bash.

"I heard through my grapevine that she's applying for a job in town."

"What? No." Bowen nearly choked on his plum. His granddad had never been one for idle conversations. And he never ever talked feelings, or speculated about their relationships so this whole standing around, not working felt weird. And where the heck were Bodhi and Beck? Bodhi'd left town before him.

"She'll get it too. Smart girl. Talented."

"Granddad, Beck's said nothing about that," Bowen said uneasily.

"I don't think he knows."

"We don't know for sure." This conversation was getting too weird, and Bowen wanted out.

His granddad looked up at him, and it struck Bowen then how many years he'd looked up physically to his granddad. Then they'd been eye-to-eye. And now he had more than an inch or two on him, and it felt wrong.

"I think Beck's in over his head. I think he's done messed up," his granddad said, and Bowen felt as if his granddad was drilling a hole in his head with his sharp gaze as if he knew something he wasn't sharing.

"Nah. He's fine." Beck had to be fine. He couldn't have both his cousins falling apart at the same time with Granddad in trouble and the future uncertain and the rodeo this weekend and finals coming up.

Bowen couldn't decide what to do with his hands. He and his granddad talked all the time, but about the ranch—what work needed to be done and who was doing what.

"I don't think she's leaving with him this time. Why should she? Life on the road's no way to be a family."

"Granddad, Ash and Beck have been together since high school. All couples have problems at one time or another," he said vaguely, feeling more uneasy. "Do you want me to talk to Beck?" he offered awkwardly.

He really wanted to talk to his granddad about what was going on with him and the ranch. He wanted to take the burden of worry from the man who had given him so much, taught him how to be a man. "Do you want me to tell him that Ashni might be applying for a job?"

"No," his granddad said. "Fool's digging his own grave, but I got to trust he'll figure it out soon enough and throw down the shovel."

His granddad made no sense. Was Bodhi right, and Granddad was ill? Stomach cramping uncomfortably now, and wishing he hadn't eaten a full breakfast, Bowen looked away, relieved when he heard the purr of a souped-up engine.

"I'll unload the truck. Bodhi's on his way up."

"He's bringing supplies. I texted him a list." His granddad widened his stance, folded his arms and squinted out across the horizon toward Copper Mountain that always seemed to act as sentry for Marietta. "Best view in the valley."

"That it is," Bowen agreed. Relieved to get off the subject of Beck and Ashni. He loved Ash like a sister and had been expecting Beck to propose for years now. Why hadn't he? None of his business, but clearly Granddad thought he should make it his. He remembered Beck's defensiveness at the Panhandle Rodeo. Clearly Beck didn't want him or Bodhi weighing in with their opinions. Not that they had any expertise, either of them. But it looked like a heart-to-heart was one more thing on his to-do list.

Bowen lowered the tailgate of his truck, needing something to do.

His granddad sat down on the truck's tailgate and sighed like he was tired. Bowen's heart lurched in alarm.

"She used to talk about med school."

Damn, they were back to Ashni again.

"Heck, so did Bodhi. But she didn't apply—waiting on Beck. Wasting her time."

Bowen pulled off his hat, ran his hand nervously through his hair and settled his straw Stetson back on his head. He'd be switching to his felt hat in another month when he came back to the ranch.

If there was a ranch to come back to.

"So many brains God gave all of you but nobody using them."

"Granddad," Bowen said urgently. He could hear Bodhi's truck getting closer and see the plume of dust kicked up by Beck's truck about a half a mile behind. "Anything you need." He put his hand on his granddad's shoulder. "Anything. We'll..."

He didn't get to finish. His granddad knocked his hand away as he stood, straight and tall beside him.

"What I need is for you boys to get to work." He swept his hand out. "I'm done," he said.

Bowen stared, shocked.

"Granddad?"

"Need you boys to spruce this place up. Got the blueprints inside the cabin. The girls hired a fancy designer for the remodel and the party. They're coming down to supervise the landscapers, but you boys are fixing up the barn and equipment shed to the specs for the party. You're also doing some kitchen upgrades and whatever else the girls want done inside the cabin so that it can be advertised as an event space and a guesthouse. I've got a list for the main house. You boys fixed up the bunkhouses last couple of breaks, so those are good to go."

"Wait, what?" Bowen stared at the massive barn where he'd snuck his first beer, kissed a girl and learned to play the guitar—hiding away from his cousins and granddad until he was good enough to not embarrass himself. He'd written his first song there up in the loft, looking at Copper Mountain through the open window where he would also toss out the bales of orchard grass and other feed to the waiting truck bed below. "An event space?"

Bowen felt like he'd been bucked off a bull and kicked in the head and then chest. He felt dazed. Nothing was making sense. His granddad was serious. He really was going to move on—sell his beloved ranch that his daddy and uncle and his granddaddy before them had hewn out a proud living.

"You heard me. Lots of rich folks looking for vacation properties in Paradise Valley. Your mom's told me all about some of her fancy high-end clients. They want the ranch without the ranch." He chuckled at his joke and headed off to his truck.

"But—" Bowen broke off as his granddad clapped him hard on his shoulder, squeezing a little, and the move was so familiar that for a moment Bowen couldn't breathe.

"Nothing lasts forever, son," Ben said softly. "Let's have one last Ballantyne Bash for the ages." He smiled, and Bowen saw the grooves radiating from his eyes to his cheeks—smile lines. He had them too, and it was like looking in a mirror fifty some years from now. Only he wouldn't be here. He wouldn't be home.

"We'll…what does Bodhi say? Pull the knob off? I think that's it. Yeah, we'll pull the knob off with this bash." He nodded and headed toward his truck. "Make it one to remember."

"Granddad." Bowen's brain raced with questions, with one argument after another. His grandfather was still healthy and active. Where was all this "the end is near" fatalism coming from? He'd never once imagined Three Tree Ranch without a Ballantyne working the land. And a wealthy celebrity or tech tycoon buying it as one more of many vacation homes and spending a week or two a year? Unthinkable.

"Now let's get unloaded and get to work." Ben opened his aged Ford F-150's tailgate with a *thunk*, clearly done with the subject Bowen wanted desperately to explore. "This year's chore list is longer than my arms because the girls had their say. Boys are here, so let's get unloaded and hand out the assignments."

BOWEN DIPPED HIS head under the showerhead for one final rinse. The hot water was heaven and now ran clean off his body, but it wasn't doing anything for the throbbing ache in his thumb on his hold hand even after two ibuprofen. He'd been distracted and disgruntled all day and now had an injury that shouldn't be that big of a deal, only a thumb was pretty crucial when trying to stick a ride. Maybe he shouldn't have played it off as nothing and iced it as both Beck and Bodhi had suggested multiple times this afternoon after he hit his thumb instead of a shingle.

Today had been a ballbuster with he and Bodhi and Beck spending all of it up on Plum Hill, cleaning out the barn and large shed, hauling loads of crap to the burn pile or landfill, stripping the walls and power washing, then getting the first coat of whitewash on the inside of both buildings. They hadn't talked much, just tried to outwork each other. Their usual camaraderie had been flat and silent. He usually enjoyed working up on roofs—he loved the view and heights had never bothered him, but now all he could think about when he saw the view—Ballantyne land spreading out what looked like forever in any direction—was that it would soon be gone.

Someone else's if he and his cousins didn't get a plan in place—a real one with a hope of success. But then thinking about how his granddad had harped on about Ashni and that the road was no place to have a family, maybe Bodhi's idea wasn't so insane.

He turned off the water and reached for a towel, his shoulders protesting a little from the hours up on the roof making repairs and then installing a massive number of hooks inside the barn and outside to hold the strings of party lights. Dang he was acting like an old man if a day of hard labor made his body protest this much.

Bodhi had cursed the project, claiming the barn would be visible from space. It had been the only laugh of the day. And one of the few times they'd spoken except about the tasks at hand. Beck had done most of the running back and forth into town for more supplies or to haul off the debris that couldn't be burned—Bowen figured he was trying to fix things with Ash, but he didn't want to ask or get in his way.

Bodhi had been on his phone more than usual and lit out a little early—likely for a date—and Beck too had mumbled an excuse and left Bowen to whitewash the last inside wall. Not that he'd minded. Langston hadn't called or texted, giving him no set plans for the evening. His granddad had a meeting with the rodeo committee, so Bowen had worked until the sun dipped behind the Gallatin Mountain range and the edges of the day had plunged into a dark and moody gray.

Still feeling unsettled despite the physical labor, Bowen had headed back to the ranch house to hit the shower, figuring Bodhi and Beck would be long gone, giving him some much-needed time to think. Only he hadn't come to any conclusions.

Was Bodhi's scheme as crazy as it seemed?

But if their granddad did want to sell his ranch, it was his right. Bowen just couldn't imagine his granddad anywhere but on the land. He'd talked about the importance of land stewardship their whole lives. He'd talked about a sense of place, of home that was in your bones. Picturing his granddad in a condo or worse, an assisted living place in Denver so that the moms could boss him, seemed unimaginable.

Maybe he's lonely.

Towel around his waist, Bowen walked to his room and wondered what to do for dinner just as his phone buzzed. Langston! He tried to ignore the way his heart did something weird even as he accepted the FaceTime call.

✪

LANGSTON SHIFTED HER weight from one foot to the other and nibbled on her lip. She hadn't quite settled on whether she wanted Bowen to answer or not.

When he answered, her breath whooshed out. "Are you naked?"

Not what she'd been planning to say, but Bowen's golden-brown hair, slicked back from his angular face, was clearly wet. And his shoulders were bare and glistened. Maybe he was working really hard and sweaty.

She crossed her legs on the barstool in the Graff bar. Shane, the bartender, was staring at her, clearly amused and intrigued. Her eyebrows arched in question.

"I have a towel on," he said as if that was somehow not more lust-inducing.

"Naked?" Shane mouthed. "Let me see."

"No," Langston clutched her phone to her chest.

"Where'd you go?" Bowen's voice was muffled.

Langston quickly pulled the phone out of what little cleavage she had. Shane laughed. Dang it. She'd stopped at the bar to check on a few things for Thursday night's specialty cocktails for the wedding rehearsal meal. The bar was fairly quiet and a good place to sit and get work done without being closed up in her office or alone in the carriage-style apartment she was renting at Walker Wilder and her husband's house. She liked Walker, and it was convenient to have her so close since the Graff event job was hers. Langston was only filling in, but she couldn't help but feel awkward. She'd met Walker when she'd been planning her own wedding. And Walker was due to have her baby any day, which, as much as Langston tried, still felt bittersweet.

The bar had seemed like a good option, but with so many of the wedding guests coming and going, it also seemed like a prime opportunity to invite Bowen. She was just a bit worried she was clinging to that excuse a little more than was valid.

"Is he naked?" Shane persisted, and Langston shook her head.

"How was your day?" she asked feeling all shades of lame. He'd said he'd help her out. She didn't need to have the breathlessness and pounding heart like she was really asking him out.

"Busy. Up on a roof or a ladder for most of it." His brow furrowed. "Preparing for the Ballantyne Bash. Granddad wants to go big this year."

"I haven't been to one of those in years," Langston said. Shoot. She sounded like she was fishing for a date. "I was wondering if you wanted to unwind…" No, she needed to make it sound casual. Not a real date, and not sexual. "Aahhh meet me at the Graff bar for a drink and appies if you're not too tired. And FlintWorks is trying out a new band tonight," she said, knowing how much Bowen loved music. She'd seen a guitar in his truck while they'd been growing up, but she'd rarely heard him play except a few times at the after bonfires with some other kids, and he stayed in the background. Did he still play?

She had to keep her focus and not moon over the past or

present Bowen Ballantyne.

"My treat," she hastened to add since he was doing her a favor—FlintWorks was on one of the suggested activity lists for the wedding guests—and she was dragging him out for a twenty-plus-minute drive into town after a long day.

"I'm paying." His voice hardened.

"Is that a yes?" Her heart soared.

"Definitive yes. I'm on my way."

She got another glimpse of his glistening chest and barely restrained her yip of happy shock.

Shane gave her a thumbs-up, and Langston mouthed *perv*.

"Tell him about the cocktail I'm making in his honor," Shane said, unrepentant for being caught peeking.

It was for the wedding and the documentary, but Bowen was fine enough to warrant his own cocktail, only she'd be making it not Shane. Langston's mood dipped a little. This was a favor. Pretend. And Bowen probably went for women like Shane who seemed ready for a good time, no strings and no hard feelings in sight, instead of her with her longing for a family so badly that she could still taste it.

"Shane is mixing up a new cocktail called Rodeo Rider, and I feel duty-bound to try it. Miranda Telford, who owns the gift shop at the Graff, is here to taste-test as well."

"Want me to hold off?"

"No, come now. I'll save you a sip."

"On my way," he said, and she could see him moving and the room blurring. She imagined him pulling the denim up his muscled thighs, over his tight ass, zipping and buttoning across his sculpted abs. Her mouth dried up.

She was definitely going to need more than a cocktail to keep herself relaxed enough to handle what tonight might hold.

✪

THE COUNTRY BAND was good. Tight. Melodic. And mixing covers with a few of their own songs. They would be one of the opening bands at the steak dinner Saturday night.

Bowen couldn't help the way his fingers moved, as if he too were picking out the notes on the neck of the guitar.

"You still play." Langston leaned close to him. Her breath feathered against his ear. "I'm glad."

He could smell her light citrus scent. Feeling a bit foolish, he looked at her, surprised that she was smiling at him.

"You do any open mics when you're on tour?"

"No. Not much," he said. "A few times with Ashni, Beck's girlfriend." He preferred writing and playing on his own.

"But you play, and I know you have an amazing singing voice. Even your speaking voice is distinctive. When we were teens, I used to try to rile you up just to hear you talk. Your voice used to give my stomach the jumps."

"That sounds bad."

"Nah. Young girls." She smiled self-deprecatingly.

"So that is why you were always in my face, riding me

hard and challenging me?"

"Guilty." She flushed a little. "I was a pain."

"I could have been nicer."

"You were a boy and a few years older." She palmed her beer glass but had yet to take a sip.

"You want something else to drink?"

"It's a brewery," she said. "I guess I'm just feeling unsettled."

"Why?"

She made a gesture toward him. "Why not? I'm just living my biggest teenage fantasy right now, and it makes me feel thrilled and stupid and guilty all at the same time."

He didn't know what to say to that. Confessing to a teen crush didn't mean that she still thought about him, right? She'd been engaged, so she was long over him. It's not like he had any confidence issues, but he didn't imagine women fantasized about him much—he'd had his share of buckle bunnies on the tour. But if Langston still had a soft spot for him, he couldn't ask her to continue the charade the following week—especially as his granddad had always had a shine for Langston when she was a girl.

A girl who had become a woman with slicked-back platinum hair, huge eyes and a white off-the-shoulder sweater with yellow stars that did spectacular things to her complexion and eyes. And her dark skinny jeans hugged her in a way that was sinful.

"I heard you playing and singing more than once," she admitted after the silence stretched out between them.

"How?" He'd done most of his playing as a kid either up in his room when his mom was at work or off on a part of the ranch where his granddad or his cousins weren't working. He loved to noodle on the guitar and write songs, but not for public consumption. Sure, his cousins knew, but no one made a big deal about it. He didn't brag that he'd sold some songs or that he was hoping to sell more to supplement the ranch—if there still was a ranch.

"I heard you playing on one of the rigs at the fairgrounds one afternoon. You'd slip away during the breaks, and I…I wondered," she admitted in a rush.

"You saying you spied on me, Langston?" He wasn't sure if he should be flattered or freaked.

"Spy sounds far more incriminating than peering around corners and hay bales." She grinned. "And I have no idea why I'm even confessing this a million years later."

"Not sure there's a statute of limitations on stalking."

"Crushing," she corrected. "And there definitely is." She slapped her hands together twice with a quick rubbing motion as if ridding herself of her past and her long-ago crush.

His chest felt warm, his limbs loose. They were adults. No longer nurturing starry-eyed dreams. He liked teasing her and getting manure flipped back at him. He liked that they had a bit of history and roots in the same town. A sense of belonging that he hadn't felt in a bar with a woman in…well, ever, settled into his bones.

This isn't real.

But when he reached out and stroked his thumb along one of her high cheekbones, it sure felt real. And he felt as alive as he did when he was lining up to go out into the arena.

"Careful, Miss Dandy. There may have been some truth serum in that rodeo cocktail the Graff bartender is experimenting with. All sorts of things might come spilling out tonight."

She smiled at him, and he jettisoned a bit more of his usual caution. "But I'll keep to the Cowboy Code." He mimed zipping his lips while she stared at him with huge eyes, and he found himself caught in their beautiful depths. While he didn't like her shorn haircut—seemed a bit too corporate to him—the boyish style did accentuate her eyes and facial structure.

"The Cowboy Code," Langston repeated slowly. "That's a great name for a drink. And a lifestyle. Shane will love that." She quickly grabbed her phone to text Shane and then she scowled as he took it away.

"Can't get the phone out on a date—even on a pretend date," he hastened to add. For some reason, with Lang, he kept relaxing. Forgetting this was just a favor, a way for her to save face.

And she could help you.

He shut down the thought. Lang was too real to pretend. His granddad would believe the charade. Even with her hair and pantsuit and inside career where she planned significant events for others while she kept in the background, she was still ranch to her bones. And that would feel too much like lying.

But what if his granddad did want to stay on his land? That was more believable than him selling up and heading meekly to Denver to split his time between his daughters.

Ben Ballantyne had a right to do what he wanted with his land, but selling it off to some tech start-up whiz or celebrity seemed so out of character. He never would have believed it but the moms were descending tomorrow. That had all of them—Bowen, Bodhi and Beck—on edge. And today as his granddad shut him down again and again hadn't helped.

Langston's phone buzzed and buzzed again. She grabbed it and texted, seeming to grow more frustrated.

"I'm sorry, Bowen. I have to go." She turned toward him suddenly, her beautiful mouth pursed like she she'd just bitten into an unripe grape. "Work." She scooted toward him, clearly expecting that one word would coax him to rise out of the chair and clear her path for escape.

"It's a bit late for that." He looked at his watch. "Nearly ten."

She sighed. "I know. It's stupid, but if I don't go now and get this over with, it will just escalate and be more unpleasant, and I really need this job and a good review."

He didn't like that at all.

"Family trouble?"

She huffed out a breath and looked away toward the band that had swung into a Keith Urban hit.

"Dang, this is one of my favorite songs." She nibbled on her lip. "Rain check?"

"You didn't answer my question."

"Still the hero." She looked down at her phone that buzzed again. "It's Mason," she admitted. "I'm sure he's just had a bit too much to drink, but he wants to talk about something. He hinted it's about the wedding plans and wants me to come up to his room."

She shifted again, as if her small hips could shift his much larger bulk, and Bowen would be lying if he didn't like the way he could feel the brief press of her breasts—even through the lapels of her jacket—against his arm.

"That sounds pretty personal to me."

"He's the one who cheated and got engaged right after, not me, so I don't think it's that."

"You don't think?"

"Bowen."

He didn't like the urgency in her voice. The tension. Or the nervousness that haunted her eyes.

"Tell him you'll meet him in your office."

"The cleaning crew is probably still there."

"In the garden in the back of the hotel."

"That's all being set up romantically for his wedding," she objected.

"All the more likely he'll remember the relationship you once had is over."

"It's too chilly to stand outside while he makes up some grievance just to make me squirm."

"I got a jacket in my truck."

"Always the white knight," she muttered.

He slid out of his chair and held out his hand to help her. Her hands were small, cold, and his reflexively closed over hers.

"I'll go with you," he said. "Stand a bit off to the side but be present." He pressed one finger over her lips. "All part of my dating services."

Chapter Seven

THINK OF YOURSELF barreling into the arena.

Langston hadn't coached herself to be strong or brave with that analogy for years, but still she found her spine snapping straight, her limbs aligning, loose but ready for action, and her jaw angled out.

"One week back in Marietta, and I'm going all cowgirl," she confessed to Bowen who walked beside her toward the doors that led to the Graff's beautiful and secluded garden off the main ballroom that had been dimly lit, the decorations still not completed for the Friday early afternoon wedding.

"I don't think the cowgirl ever went away," Bowen said. He slipped his arm around her—warm, strong and reassuring, when she shouldn't want those things at all.

Favor.

Pretend.

But Bowen was very real, and the attraction she figured would have been long gone by distance, maturity, and grief was a pulse in her blood.

"Nervous?"

"No," she snapped. She wasn't nervous about meeting

Mason. But the way Bowen opened doors for her as if it were the most natural thing in the world, and draped his denim jacket over her shoulders so that now she inhaled his masculine scent with every breath, sent her nerves firing into a meltdown.

"Annoyed," she substituted, although it was a lot more than that, if she were being honest, which she wasn't particularly eager to be.

She was so aware of him. Her skin tingled, like it wanted to roll off of her and onto him.

Down, girl.

Sometimes a vivid imagination was a hindrance.

"I'll stay close," Bowen promised.

She opened her mouth to tell him not to bother, when Mason rose up from a bench where he'd been typing something furiously on his phone.

"What took you so long?" he demanded. "Seriously?" He looked at Bowen.

"What did you want to discuss, Mason?" Langston kept her voice low and soothing.

Bowen looked like he wanted to clock the irritated expression off Mason's face. Seeing the two men side by side was disconcertingly eye-opening. Mason, blond and handsome and suited up, looked like he had just finished a long photo shoot depicting a businessman's night on the town. And Bowen looked like he'd walked out of every dream she'd ever had.

"Did you want to discuss the hot-air ballooning activity

tomorrow morning? The hike? The kayak tour? The horseback riding and outdoor cookout? Wedding details?"

Bowen stared at her as if shocked by the list. It was fairly comprehensive. Mason's family didn't do anything small and Langston knew all that Marietta had to offer.

"I'd prefer to discuss this in private," Mason said.

Why was he behaving like this? He hadn't even granted her a private audience when she had to tell him about their loss or to discuss his cheating or pregnant girlfriend or her firing. Irritation nipped at her heels, but she breathed in on a count of four and out. She needed this job.

She touched Bowen's arm, letting her fingers curl around his strength.

"This will just be a minute," she said, not wanting to completely capitulate to Mason, and then she wanted to kick her own behind. Bowen was doing her a favor. He wasn't really a man who cared for her or her safety or her emotional reactions any more than he would for an average woman, she reminded herself. He'd helped Shauna get home safely. She wasn't any more special.

"I'll wait," Bowen said, facing her, leaning over her a little as if sheltering her. His hands cupped her face for a moment. "I'll be right over there, and then we can go for that drive we were talking about."

The warmth in his eyes belied the seriousness of his expression. Langston felt like he'd cast some magical spell to mesmerize her. They hadn't discussed a drive, but now Langston found herself longing for just that—climbing in his truck, cranking up the tunes and taking a long, random drive—hopefully, with a make-out session at the end of the road.

She'd dreamed of a date like that with Bowen as a teen. She was an adult now and shouldn't be harboring any girlish fantasies.

"Yes, please," she said meaning it. "I'd like that." She stood on her tiptoes to kiss his cheek to thank him for everything—pulling her fully out of the shadows of her past few months.

He kissed her lips, soft but lingering. "Take care of business," he said. And then he stepped away. "And then we'll head out."

"That was sweet," Mason groused, sounding like he was choking. "Makes me wonder if I was too trusting while you and my mother planned for this dragged-out, over-the-top, western-themed exorbitant wedding."

"You too trusting?" she repeated, too shocked to not take the bait. "What's that supposed to mean? You were the one banging my cousin in the house I bought and designed for us."

He waved his hand as if his fidelity was irrelevant. "Keep your voice down." Mason looked around uneasily. "If you hadn't lied about the baby…" The rest of what he had planned to say degenerated into a gurgled hiss as Langston hurtled the few feet separating them and slugged him in the jaw. He yelped and hunched, and she kneed him in the balls.

"Are you insane?" he hissed looking up at her from a

crouched position.

"I almost died," she bit out. "And you weren't there."

Then Bowen was, gently enfolding her in his arms while he handed Mason his handkerchief that he'd dipped in the fountain.

"You should get some ice on that," he said, one hand soothing circles on her back while Langston glared at Mason, shaking with adrenaline and ready to go for round two. His teeth must have cut his lip a little, because as he dabbed at his mouth, his expression shocked and furious and edged with pain, the handkerchief came away pink with a little blood.

"To hell with ice. I'm calling the cops. You're out of control."

"Mason." Langston, fury and hurt still screaming through her, made a grab at sanity. She couldn't lose this job. She couldn't.

"You call the sheriff," Bowen said conversationally. "The press may twig onto it. Logan Tate, a friend of mine, likes headlines."

Mason stiffened.

"You're bluffing."

"You're not worth my time. I googled you while you were strutting around in a pathetic power play, Mr. Montana wannabe. I wonder..." Bowen crossed his arms and leaned against the base of the fountain as if he did this every night, and for all she knew, maybe he did. "What the press would make of you sneaking around and cheating on your fiancée with her cousin and then getting beaten up by a girl? Do Montana voters want that in their leader?"

Langston opened her mouth to object to the girl statement, but Bowen shifted slightly, and his thumb drifted across her lower lip. "I like that you're tough and can take care of your own business."

She settled a little, but fury and mortification still swept through her.

Mason's face turned a dull red.

"Baby, why don't you get some ice for Mason?" Bowen turned her around and nudged her toward the door. "Don't want any bruises in the wedding photos—or are they campaign shots?"

Langston started to shake, and despite Bowen's jacket, she felt cold. How could she go from hot fury to icy trembles within a minute? Admitting that Bowen was in better control than she was, and needing a moment to pull herself together, she hurried to the Graff's kitchen, hoping to grab some ice without fielding any questions from the bar staff.

She heard Bowen's deep, calm drawl the minute she opened the door.

"Why did you want to talk to Langston alone?"

"I wanted to make sure she was okay." Mason sounded a little whiny.

"Try again."

"Who the hell do you think you are? You googled me so you know who I am. You know about my political ambitions. My family. You don't want me for an enemy."

"We don't need to be enemies." Bowen sounded totally reasonable as if he and Mason had met casually at a party. "I just want you to know that Langston isn't alone. She's making a new life for herself."

"With you?" Mason sneered.

"Here's the ice, Mason." Langston couldn't stand to hide in the dark, allowing Bowen to take any of Mason's shoveled crap.

She knew she should apologize for hitting him, but the words stuck in her throat. All the grief and loneliness during the past few months had just rushed over her, making her feel like she was still sucked out to sea, struggling back toward shore. Like she would lie about something like that—losing their child. Nearly dying from blood loss and an infection.

"Fifteen minutes on and off at least a few times tonight," Bowen said calmly.

"What, you get in a lot of fist fights?" Mason demanded, his voice seethed with resentment.

"My tussles are more with bulls," Bowen said. "You haven't told Langston why you needed to see her alone."

Mason was pissed. "I just wanted to make sure that she wasn't going to cause problems and mess up the wedding plans."

"Like you did?"

"You don't know the whole story."

"Man cheats on the woman he promised to love and honor and build a life with is all I need to know."

"You're nothing but a cowboy. Thousands of them all over Montana."

"Isn't that the whole point of the western-themed wedding?" Bowen didn't take offense. He seemed more amused. "To cowboy up? Be a man of the land, the heritage? Make yourself more appealing to a wider swatch of Montana voters?"

Mason shifted the ice but kept it on his lip.

"I just want the wedding over with and without any drama or bad press."

"I have no intention of doing anything to wreck your wedding," Langston objected. "I worked for your mother for seven years. I'm a professional. I've never had any complaints—all positive reviews, and yet she fired me while I was still in the hospital after my miscarriage—and you'd told your family we'd broken up and you'd fallen in love with Sheila, who was expecting the next scion."

She could feel Bowen's shock and rising tension. Way to spill her dirty laundry, and she didn't even have the self-control to keep the hurt and bitterness out of her voice.

"She shouldn't have fired you," Mason finally said as if that were the critical, most painful point. "I told her not to do that, but she wanted a clean break. And then you were here. Supervising our wedding. Seemed like too big of a coincidence to believe."

Bowen shifted and linked his fingers with hers, and for a moment her eyes burned. How nice it would be to have a friend. To have support. To not have to fight everything alone. She'd lost so much, but no one had grieved with her. Told her they were sorry. Visited her in the hospital. Held her when she learned her baby had died before it got to live.

She took a shaky breath to keep herself in the present, in reality, not a fantasy—the fantasy she'd harbored with Mason, the man with the big family, belonging, a life with big plans.

But she now knew she didn't fit in that life. She breathed in finally feeling free.

"Marietta is my hometown, Mason. You knew that. I lost my job. You and Sheila decided to keep the house that we bought, and you wouldn't give me back my earnest money or part of the deposit. I had no job, no home, no family and my savings depleted. You knew all of that." She crossed her arms and glared. "You and your mother left me with no options in Missoula or Helena so don't act surprised that I jumped at the first gig I could get no matter where it was or how distasteful, and don't think I'd lower myself by not putting on a spectacular, flawless event. After all, I planned it, and now I'm executing it. There is no way I will let a high-profile wedding reflect poorly on the Graff or me."

She took a step toward him, nearly vibrating with the intensity of her feelings and was pleased when his eyes flared in alarm and he took a step back.

"Your wedding will be charming, entertaining, and stunning for everyone attending, providing you and your guests a spectacular week of activities and memories and plenty of breathtaking footage for your campaign ads."

"All positive," Mason hissed.

"Mason, I have no sway or control over your emotions or actions. You made that clear months ago. Besides," she said, "a little fear and uncertainty add spice to life."

✪

"I WISH I'D hit him again," Langston said the minute Bowen parked his truck, headlights shining through the evergreens to reveal a glimmer of Miracle Lake beyond. She didn't really remember him walking her to his truck, only that he had, and then he'd said they'd go for a drive.

She'd needed that—to get away, to calm down, to be away from people while she pulled herself together.

Of course he'd remember that she'd twice told him Miracle Lake was her favorite place to come to think—only she hadn't come here at night. It was beautiful, ethereal but a little spooky. She kept waiting for some creature to come charging out of the heavily wooded shoreline.

"Still wishing I'd popped him a hard one-two punch myself," Bowen said.

Langston made a fist and wiggled her fingers. "I hit him hard. It hurts a bit," she admitted now that Bowen had stopped his truck and silence and dark descended.

He took her hand in his and looked at it. "Should have saved some of that ice for yourself."

She tried to ignore the warmth that tingled through her at his touch and his closeness. He was just being Bowen:

kind, responsible, helping to champion another's cause even though he didn't have to.

"Did you tuck your thumb?"

"Yup." She grinned up at him. "Just like you showed me how to throw a punch when I was what, eight or nine, and the other kids were merciless about my hair and well, about my everything back then."

"Makes me wish you'd hit him harder, Lang."

"He would have whined about it. Made trouble, and I…I really need to start acting my age."

"I'm sorry he hurt you," Bowen said, as Langston stared out across the black water, lit only by the half-moon and a billion stars. She didn't know what to say. Of course Bowen was sorry on her account. Probably mad for her. Why hadn't she fallen in love with a man like Bowen? Why hadn't he stuck around to be fallen in love with?

The quiet enveloped the truck, and it felt peaceful. Safe.

"I'm sorry you lost your baby," he said. His hand rested on her shoulder and then traced down her arm, and despite the fact that she'd been holding herself together for so long, and there was a large console between them, she turned her face into his shoulder and threw her arms around his neck.

She didn't blubber like a baby exactly, but the tears were hot and fast and building up to a headache before she started sucking in one shaky breath after another.

He didn't say anything else, just rubbed slow circles on her back, and she breathed him in.

"I had a daughter," she said. "A baby girl, and the doctor

said that she stopped developing around thirteen weeks, but I'm the only one who grieves her."

"Lang, losing a child at any age, any stage is a terrible loss."

She nodded. "The baby was so real to me, and I was so excited to start on a family. Mason was mad. Accused me of jumping the gun or getting pregnant so that we'd get married and then, by the time the wedding arrangements were started with the wedding planner and…and at my next doctor's appointment there was no heartbeat, and he accused me of making it up."

Bowen reared away from her and glared out the window. She felt the loss of his warmth and touch all the way to her marrow.

"And he was traveling and didn't come back, so I was alone when the miscarriage started, and I was so scared and I didn't stop bleeding, and then later I got an infection and was septic, and still he…"

"Alone?" His voice sounded like a bullet from a gun.

She nodded, wanting to shut up but somehow, here in the dark, miles from town at the lake where she'd spent winters ice-skating and more than a few summer days swimming after barrel racing practice, she wanted to get it out—all of it. Maybe then she could finally start again.

Poor Bowen. He'd always been the shoulder girls would cry on—usually about Bodhi.

"I didn't know what to do. It hurt worse than the doctor said it would. And I still went to work, but I started getting sicker and sicker. I passed out at work and was sent to a hospital."

Bowen didn't move. His face could have been carved in the granite spearing up from the tectonic plates.

"Say something."

"Better I don't."

"Do. Mason said I was melodramatic or trying to make my lie more believable. His mom said something was wrong with the baby and the miscarriage was a blessing and then she said…she said something might be wrong with me after…that I might not be able to have healthy children."

The tic in his jaw surprised her. She'd never noticed that before, and she'd done a lot of Bowen-gazing in her youth.

"And then he cheated on you."

"That wasn't the first time," she admitted. "Since Sheila was so quick to announce her pregnancy."

She'd never told anyone any of this—that Mason accused her of making up the baby. And then he cheated with her cousin—her assistant—and got her pregnant. She could still see them on the bed that she'd spent too much time carefully choosing. Langston swallowed the bile in her throat and leaned back against the seat.

"I'd met Walker at an event planning conference, and she called me to see if I knew anyone who could cover for her for a year's maternity leave so I came home." She closed her eyes. "Even though Marietta isn't home."

"It's your home, Lang. It will always be home."

"Doesn't feel like it." But she'd done enough whining for

a lifetime.

"I thought it would be a great place to restart. Plan my next move. Rise. Phoenix from the ashes and all that."

"And then what?"

"I don't know. The job is for a year. I don't think I'll stay."

"Why not?"

"Too many memories. Hard to reinvent yourself when everyone thinks they know you."

Bowen was quiet. What were his plans after he retired from rodeo? She couldn't imagine him not on Three Tree Ranch with his cousins and granddad.

"Do you have any blankets in the truck?"

"Of course."

He was a cowboy. Stupid question.

"Are all of them horse blankets?"

"Not all," he drawled. "You're not thinking about—?"

She didn't give him the time to finish the question. She kicked off her boots, opened the door and shed his jacket.

"Lang, that's glacier fed," she heard him call out behind her, as if she didn't know. But she felt like she needed this. An icy plunge. A shock to her system. A cleanse. A chilly late-night baptism to be born again.

She peeled off her skirt and let it hit the dirt, and then ripped off her tank and let it flutter to the ground. She ran the last few steps in her bra and panties and cleaved into the water.

✪

DAMN, SHE WAS beautiful. All white, smooth, tight lines. Graceful. Coordinated. An athlete. He grabbed two Pendleton blankets from the back of his cab and walked down to the water's edge, finding himself holding his breath until she surfaced with a primal shriek.

"It's cold!"

She looked like a lake nymph—were there any of those? If so, Montana's alpine lakes is where they would reside and fuel cowboys' dreams.

"Is that so?"

"I don't remember it being this cold when we were kids."

"We were dumber then."

She continued to tread water, looking at him holding the blankets.

"C'mon in now," he urged shaking the blanket out a little as if he were a matador coaxing a reluctant bull.

"It's really, really cold."

"Said everyone, always." She didn't respond. "Don't make me swim out there. Then we'll both be cold."

"Close your eyes."

He barely managed to keep the smirk off his face, but dutifully closed them, wanting her out of the water. While the night wasn't too chilly, she'd get hypothermic in the water pretty quickly, especially someone as small and slim as she was. He was already wishing he'd turned on the heater in his truck on high before he'd left to retrieve her.

He felt her approach and as she took one of the blankets, and he opened his eyes. Her lips already blue and teeth chattering. He toweled her off briskly even though she slapped at his hands a little. He bundled her up in the second blanket like a burrito and carried her back to the truck, turning it on and letting the heat go full blast. Then he retrieved her clothes, folded them and put them carefully in her lap.

"Feel better?" he asked after he got back in his truck.

"This might seem strange," she said, still chattering and clutching the blanket close. "But actually I do. I feel like I got rid of everything I've been holding in so tightly—like I washed it away. Like I can be me again."

He didn't respond. He thought of everything he too held in so tightly. Could he let it all go? Wash himself clean. Was it that easy to cleanse the past and start over? Rebuild his life? Create a new future perhaps far from Marietta, far from family, cut himself adrift?

Everything inside him rebelled at that idea.

But it might be necessary. His mom and aunts had applied pressure and guilt his entire life to manipulate him. He couldn't wait to get out of the house and be his own man. He didn't want to try to guilt his granddad into holding on to the ranch if his granddad really wanted to let it go.

But why was it so impossible to believe Ben Ballantyne would ever leave his ranch, the only home he'd ever known, in the town and state he was so proud of? Was that just wishful thinking?

Bowen drove her back to town, neither of them talking. Lang finally stirred as he turned off the highway for Marietta. She shimmied back into her skirt and tank and slipped her feet into her shoes.

"I know another less drastic, less chilly way to find your way back to yourself," he said as he pulled up to the house where she was renting a guest cottage.

"I'm sure you do." She grinned at him, and his gut that had been churning settled a little.

He turned off the truck and turned to face her.

Her expression was curious, a little wary, eyes huge in her heart-shaped face. The ends of her cropped hair were beginning to dry from the long blast of heat that had made him start to sweat long before they'd hit town. He could see the beginnings of the curls, the short fluff, and it took a lot of concentration to not try to wrap one of those tight curls around his finger.

"Ride with me one day," he said. "Come out to the ranch."

"Bowen." She hesitated.

He cupped her face. "Ride with me. Please."

Her expression searched his, and he wondered what she was looking for, and if she'd find it. He felt like he was holding his breath, and then she seemed to relax a little as if some air had escaped, leaving her more pliant.

"Okay," she said. "Wednesday afternoon might work," she said hesitantly. She arched up and kissed his cheek. And then she reached for the door handle.

"No," was all he said, and he was out of the truck and around the hood and opening her door.

"The Cowboy Code," he said, hoping to make her smile again.

And when she did, Bowen felt something in his chest stir, and for a moment it felt like that little forgotten piece of something might just take flight.

Instead he stomped it down and walked her to her door, waited while she unlocked it, but she didn't go inside or close the door. She waited at the entrance, gold light spilling out around her and waited while he walked back to his truck. She waved and slipped inside, and he stared at the closed door.

She was local. But not planning to stay in Marietta. Still, she was vulnerable. She'd been badly hurt. She wanted permanent. And he was not a man built for long term.

And maybe that was why his granddaddy was giving up on him.

On all of them.

Chapter Eight

LANGSTON WALKED THROUGH one set of the French doors in the ballroom and out into the garden. It buzzed with activity. Gardeners and staff and also a crew from a local landscaping company as well as the local florist, Sweet Pea Designs, had turned the garden into a wonderland of white roses, with a few pale pink roses woven into the floral arch.

She took several pictures for the Graff's event portfolio. Not that many events were this lavish, but with Walker Wilder's hard work, and to be honest, hers over the past few months when she'd been planning her own wedding, the garden was transformed into an elegant floral fantasy straight out of a fairy tale.

She'd expected to feel a stab of regret or sorrow—something.

Instead, she felt renewed. Chapter closed. Book returned. Another checked out.

This morning felt like the fresh start she'd been looking for after her icy dip in Miracle Lake. Maybe she'd had her own small miracle—her grief and humiliation washed away.

Pouring herself another large coffee from the catering

station, Langston consulted her notes. She walked the perimeter of the garden and where the bridal group would congregate tomorrow, and then she checked the seating. The bunting was still being tied to the chairs, but the accent flowers would be added tomorrow morning.

The color-coded tape had been set down for the camera crew and the wedding photographer. The garden setting would be perfect for tomorrow afternoon's rehearsal lunch. And then the women of the bridal party were going to have a spa afternoon while the men fished and kayaked.

Now for the ballroom. Yesterday, the state of disarray might have worried her, but even in the week she'd been here, she'd come to trust and respect the small staff. "We are small but mighty," she murmured, making claws with her hand holding the coffee and growling under her breath.

The preparations were proceeding smoothly even though Mason's mother spit out change orders like cherry pits. Luckily, her aunt Lucy was too intimidated by the wealth and arrogance of Mason's family and thrilled that her daughter had caught their precious son to form an opinion about anything except gushing approval.

Also keeping her calm under pressure was the fact that Langston had been planning events since college. She was smart, creative, diplomatic and confident. She'd needed each one of those skills this week.

But now a reprieve loomed since the wedding party, film crew, and guests were off site this afternoon and tomorrow after the rehearsal. Langston returned outside to the garden and spotted Sheila clutching Mason's sleeve, her mouth down in a pout and her blue eyes drenched in tears. It gave Langston no pleasure to see him wave away Sheila's concern.

Been there. Done that.

"I'm hoping you still have time for a break later today?" a very familiar deep voice whispered in her ear.

Her heart jumped and raced and even though she mentally called it back it did a little two-step out of its protected gate.

Bowen stood next to her, holding a vibrant bouquet of daisy varietals.

"I want to tempt you with lunch."

"Oh, um, like grab something at the diner?" she asked, trying to quash some of her excitement at seeing him. On Monday night he'd mentioned taking her to the ranch. Part of her was dying to go, the other part was afraid to open that Pandora's box of her past.

"I had something else in mind." And the way her imagination took off after that comment was darn right sinful.

"I'm listening."

He leaned closer to her, and she looked up at him.

Bowen Ballantyne is going to kiss me.

Her heart raced, and her lips parted.

"Are they watching?" he asked.

"Who?" And then color flooded her face. He was trying to help her out, show Mason and her cousins that she wasn't heartbroken. And she was acting like she was sixteen and crushing all over again.

His mouth was so close to her, she felt the puff of air when he spoke. "Have lunch with me."

"I…" She couldn't look away from him even if she'd had a leash and collar and someone jerked it.

"I have it on good authority that today there are a variety of activities for guests to enjoy, and tomorrow is ladies' spa day."

"Good authority?"

He grinned, and she felt his charm to her toes.

"My ability to read your notes in the lobby. You worked late last night. Tomorrow morning is an absurdly early start. What are you trying to do, keep rancher hours? Have lunch with me. You know you want to." He nuzzled her ear. "Dandelion," he whispered.

She made a mock fist. "That's it, Ballantyne," she challenged.

He laughed at her. Laughed. And then he caught her fist and kissed her knuckles. One by one, his eyes reading hers, and really what other answer was there but yes?

"I THINK THIS is another Ballantyne bait and switch," Langston said as Bowen pulled up outside the main barn.

"Where would you get an idea like that?"

"You offered me lunch." Langston watched several horses trotting around a large arena move closer to the fence. "I should have suspected when you suggested I change out of business gear."

"I got lunch covered." Bowen swung himself out of the truck.

For a moment she allowed her mind to go there—yes, she did. Bowen, shirt off, golden, his body blanketing hers, his sun-kissed skin warm under her fingers, his mouth moving over hers, taking control, making her forget her own name.

"Ride with me?" Bowen asked persistently, now opening her side of the truck, holding out his hand. "You know you want to."

She did. And the strength of her longing stole her breath.

"I haven't in a while," she confessed in a rush. "I didn't want to. I thought it would be too disloyal to Buttercup and too hard for me."

She waited for him to tell her that her concerns were stupid. Mason would have. Her granddad would have dismissed her feelings as well. A horse was a horse. A tool. But Bowen's blue-gray gaze was steady, kind, and his mouth carried a hint of a smile.

"Horses are special," he said, "especially those we compete and win and lose with."

She'd known, just known, he'd understand.

"Time to dust off your inner cowgirl and make some new memories."

It was long past time. She took his hand and followed Bowen to the corral where she stepped up on the first rung and listened while he introduced the horse she would ride.

He had an apple and carrot piece for each in his pocket. It was such a natural thing, and the tears that stung her eyes were unacceptable. Thankful for her sunglasses, she reached out to scratch Blue Velvet's neck.

"You really haven't ridden since you left for college?" Bowen asked, looking sideways at her.

She avoided his too-discerning scrutiny by turning more fully toward Blue Velvet. If it was one thing about cowboys—and cowgirls—they could read body language in animals. And humans weren't as mysterious as they wished.

Of course, Bowen knew how to wait for an answer. Time to stop being a coward.

"Granddad sold the last few parcels of the ranch during my first semester of college. Sold the livestock, including all the horses, at auction, which financed his retirement, paid off my dad's debts for the last time, and gave me some money toward tuition and living expenses for my first year."

"But you were on a rodeo scholarship."

"I had to give it up because he sold Buttercup."

That dropped like a grenade with the pin still in. She felt like she should defend her granddad when she didn't want to. But it had been his ranch. His life had been stuffed with disappointment and sorrow. His two daughters had moved away and his precious, talented son had too many troubles to count. She also felt she should shrug off her father's mistakes because everyone else did—business schemes that failed, the drinking, womanizing, gambling, broken promises.

Langston breathed in the dirt and animal and grass and

sun and man and finally felt home.

"Let's take that ride, cowboy." She smiled.

"Saddle up, cowgirl," he leaned in to whisper in her ear. Just what she wanted to hear. "If you remember how."

And then Bowen Ballantyne winked at her and sauntered into the barn, clearly knowing he was the hottest cowboy in all of Montana if not all of the western ranches.

How easily the practiced movements came back! She was a little stiff, a little slower, but her gym workouts had kept her strong enough that she didn't stagger under the weight of the saddle Bowen handed her.

He smoothed the saddle blanket over Blue Velvet, who kept nuzzling his pocket for more treats.

"Greedy," Bowen chastised cheerfully.

But Langston was on the horse's side. Bowen was utterly tempting, and she couldn't blame Blue Velvet for seizing the opportunity to nuzzle.

"Need some help?" Bowen asked as she walked toward Blue Velvet, flipping up one stirrup to rest on the saddle while she lifted it up and over.

"Not totally a city girl," she huffed.

She'd always been fiercely independent and hadn't let her petite size or gender hold her back, and she wasn't about to start now. Sure, she'd been knocked down, but she'd jumped back up swinging and she was going to find her joy again.

Langston cinched the saddle as Bowen eyeballed her work, pretending he wasn't, which would have pissed her off with anyone else, but the chance to breathe him in, feel his body heat and have his fingers touching hers was too good to pass up.

"Hey, cuz, looks like great minds think alike."

Langston straightened along with Bowen and found Bodhi entering the barn with Nico by his side.

"Or we're both dodging the moms, who think it a great sport to see who has the longest list of chores for us to accomplish," Bodhi added.

Bowen didn't bite conversationally or smile. But Nico did. She stepped forward and re-introduced herself.

As if anyone would ever forget her even if they had a head injury.

She was so tall and beautiful that really, Langston should have hated her on sight. But Nico had a luminous smile that lit up the room, and her green eyes even with the exotic thick and extended line of her eyeliner seemed to radiate friendliness and spunk through all the glamour of her thick, wavy auburn hair and new, designer clothing. Her boots were Frye's, and her black skinny jeans fit like skin.

"Bodhi's going to 'teach' me to ride," Nico said using air quotes.

"I hope that's not a euphemism," Langston said.

"That might be his plan." Nico laughed. Bodhi didn't and Nico hip-checked him. "Lighten up. You said you were the fun one."

"I am." Bodhi smiled tightly.

"I packed us a picnic. That Monroes' Grocery Store may be small, but it is well stocked, and I love how many local products are featured. And I bought sandwiches and cookies from the Java Café so we got plenty of food. You two should join us."

Langston opened her mouth to agree. Nico seemed nice, and perhaps by riding and picnicking with the other couple, she'd stop torturing herself by lusting after a noble man who was only doing her a favor. She was rebuilding her life, not knocking it back down again.

Although, would a fling with Bowen be such a bad thing?

He's hotter than the sun.

You'd get scorched.

Best way to shake a broken heart—jump on a new horse.

He made his lack of interest in you clear years ago.

Her bad angel and good angel argued while Bowen finally spoke up.

"Thank you for the invitation." He smiled as Bodhi stiffened, his expression hardening. "But Langston has time for only a short ride."

Bodhi snorted at that, and Langston out of longtime habit kicked Bodhi's shin.

Dandelion, he mouthed, and grinned at her, utterly unrepentant.

She stuck her tongue out like she was ten again.

"I'm working," Langston reminded Bodhi.

"Is that what they call it?"

What was up with him? Langston looked up at Bowen searching for answers to the tension she could feel snaking through the barn and wrapping around both Ballantynes. Bowen and his cousins' tightness was legendary. Fight one, take them all on.

"Bowen's a dark horse," Bodhi said. "You and he have that chat yet, Langston?"

How was it possible that that random question cranked Bowen's tension higher? Bodhi's tight smile and glittering navy eyes seemed like some sort of victory Langston didn't understand.

"Yes." She jumped fully on board with team Bowen. "We've discussed everything and have our plan in place."

She could read Bodhi and Bowen enough to realize some sort of game or challenge was on, and her competitive spirit lit. Why should Bodhi think he had the win in his column? Bowen had really stepped up for her this week. She could do him a solid. All he had to do was tell her what he needed.

"And you know me, Bodhi. I always play to win."

"I remember." Bodhi's smile went full wattage. "Not sure you haven't bitten off more than you can chew, cuz," he said to Bowen.

Bowen didn't answer. Of course not. The quiet one who led with his actions not his mouth.

"We got this," Langston said brashly having no idea what 'this' was. Bowen definitely had some explaining to do. She swung herself up on Blue Velvet. "See you at the finish line, Bodhi, prize in our hands."

LANGSTON GAVE BLUE Velvet her lead to run. Not that Bowen had been worried that so many years had passed since she'd ridden, but clearly her body remembered. And reveled. He wasn't sure who enjoyed the freedom of the full gallop more, Langston or Blue Velvet. Finally she slowed Blue to more of a trot and patted her neck. The beauty of the afternoon, the sun, the vivid blue sky, and the miles of wheat-colored grass waving in the slight breeze, all of it a backdrop to the woman who looked like a pagan sun-worshipping goddess nearly overwhelmed him.

"It's been too long," Langston shouted to the sky, dropping the reins to drape over the horse's midnight-black neck and mane.

"Why?" Bowen let his horse come up alongside hers. "Surely, you must have friends who had horses and some land."

"Not in college really," she said. "Granddaddy moved to Tucson. He had a sister out there and some friends. I was on my own and college isn't cheap. If I wasn't studying on campus, I was working at my off-campus job in a sandwich shop. Not much time for fun."

Bowen nodded. "Speaking of sandwiches, you good for a bit more of a ride before we tuck in to the lunch I packed?"

"I'm good to ride," she said. "I've missed it even though I tried to not think about horses or the rodeo or Marietta for so long. Are we going to talk before or after we eat?"

Damn.

"We're talking."

"Right." Langston screwed up her face comically. He'd forgotten how animated she was. "You know what I mean—whatever Bodhi was taunting us about."

Us? He'd only been an us with his cousins, and he tried to swat away the rush of warmth that filled him.

"That game or challenge or whatever I just committed us to," she said.

"No commitment," he said quickly without thinking. She didn't need any more drama or men playing games with her heart or her life.

It was like watching a light go off. Her face shuttered. Her energy dimmed. Bowen wanted to kick himself.

"Got it," she said and gave Blue Velvet her head and tapped the horse into another gallop.

Dammit. Maybe there was no way to play it safe. Maybe he couldn't protect all of them—his granddad, cousins and Lang. Maybe there was no win for any of them.

But Langston at least deserved the truth.

THEY RODE IN silence. Langston willed her emotions back under control. So he didn't want to talk. What was new? She'd always been on the outside looking in. No big deal. Bowen had agreed to do her a solid. He didn't owe her anything beyond that. He would be back on the road after next weekend, and she would be fine without him.

She wasn't going to allow anything to interfere with the gorgeous day and the pleasure of riding Blue Velvet.

Bowen steered off to the left, and she followed. The land rose up here—not too high, but she could see a lot of granite boulders sticking up and a few scattered oak trees. The beauty and topographical diversity on Three Tree Ranch was truly spectacular.

"Your family has such a gorgeous spread, Bowen," she said, swinging down from Blue Velvet when he stopped. "Is it hard to leave after a visit?"

"Yes." He pulled out a small chilled cooler bag from one of the saddle satchels. "I always feel like I'm home the minute we head down the mountain on Highway 89."

"How often do you come back?" She could do this. Keep the conversation from veering into the personal. She led the horses to the shade of one of the trees and pulled out a few apple slices Bowen had given her earlier. Their velvety noses tickling her palm was soothing.

"Every chance we get. We come for the long break between the tour and finals every year, two weeks in September for the rodeo and bash, and then stay the week after to help out. And then usually one or all of us will come during our weeks off. Take off some load so Granddad doesn't have to hire more hands."

"It's beautiful. Do you bring all your lunch dates here?" She winced at the edge in her voice. She had no right to feel jealous. None. Bowen wasn't on offer. She needed to rebuild her life and confidence and then she would find a man who wanted to build a life and family with her—a man who would stay.

"Haven't brought a woman home to the ranch."

"Really?" She found that hard to believe.

"There's a blanket in the other saddle bag."

Langston retrieved it, looked around at the view and the ground, and chose a spot in the shade.

"Thank you for today, Bowen." She focused on spreading out the orange, red and light brown plaid blanket. "I've tried to forget how much I loved riding, working with horses and putting them through their paces and being on a ranch. My life is so different now, but today felt good." She finally let the blanket settle so that she could meet his searching gaze.

"Our ride's not over yet."

She nodded. "Blue Velvet is a treasure." She looked at the horse, not him. "Thank you for sharing her with me today."

Her eyes burned. This would not do. Langston pasted on her best prickly customer-wrangling smile. "And now I find myself famished and looking forward to judging your lunch-making skills."

"I've been on my own a long while and like to eat. I think I'll pass muster."

He brought the food and two Hydro Flasks gleaming with icy condensation of something that was going to be very welcome. Her mouth dried as she watched him approach—lean cowboy who looked so masculine and sexy.

She sat down, pulled her legs in tailor style and enjoyed the view of the sun haloing him as he dropped down beside her with the athletic grace that, for her anyway, epitomized the moves of a rodeo cowboy.

"Thank you!" She took out a cutting board and helped to lay out the spread: several pre-cut sandwiches, fruit, chopped veggies and chips. "You went all out." She tried to not feel touched, but she did. She was also confused. "Why?"

"Why?" he echoed as he sat down next to her and Langston felt trapped into the beautiful and thoughtful depths of his gray-blue gaze. It was like falling back into the Marietta wormhole of her teen dreams. "Why not?" He leaned forward and closed the distance between them.

She dropped the bell pepper and the pocketknife she'd been planning to slice the pepper with.

His lips were warm, firm, and shockingly persuasive. Langston had been urging herself to play it cool, to not care that he wasn't coming clean with her, but with one touch of his lips, all her caution evaporated. She breathed him in, parted her lips and let his tongue explore the inner seam of her top lip, which sent sparks throughout her body.

"You really know how to kiss," she said shakily when they paused, both needing air. It could have been ten minutes or an hour.

"I've been wanting to do that for longer than I care to admit," he said. So had she! Langston reached for him to pull him closer, her entire body aching and humming for more, but after a brief, warm kiss, he rested his forehead against hers.

She could feel his heart slam against hers.

It's just physical. It's just sex.

But it felt like so much more.

"I think we should talk before we go any further."

She'd wanted to talk earlier, but the way Bowen said it sounded ominous.

"Yes," she said grabbing for a restraint she wasn't sure she wanted. "I know this thing between us is pretend…"

"Lang," he interrupted, tangling his fingers in her cropped hair and frowning as it was so stiff with product to try to keep her curls flat.

God, why had she cut her hair again? She'd had a lot of dumb impulses in her life, but that one had been the stupidest—second only to ripping off her shirt and trying to climb in Bowen's truck when she'd been sixteen.

"You're doing me a favor." She tried to bring her rioting thoughts under a semblance of control. "I get that, but I…I don't know what we're doing here." She gestured to him, the lunch, the scenery. "I'm grateful. I am…but…"

"I didn't do it for your gratitude," Bowen bit out.

How had she pissed him off when she was trying to give him an out?

"Mason isn't here. None of my family or colleagues are here so we don't need to pretend."

Bowen pulled away and sat across from her out of touching range. She could see a muscle tick in his jaw, and it was thrilling and sexy.

"Pretending," Bowen finally said, his arms on his thighs, hands dangling tanned and work-rough over his knees. "I'm not good at it. The lines are starting to blur for me."

She sucked in a quick breath. What did that mean? Was he attracted to her even a tiny bit?

"We're both adults," Langston said far more calmly than she felt.

"I'm trying to behave here, Lang, and you are not helping." The look he shot her went straight to her core.

"Maybe I don't want to," she whispered.

"You've been hurt," he said. His eyes went darker with the seriousness of the topic. "Betrayed. You suffered a loss no woman should have to endure. I don't want to add on to that."

Lang could barely swallow. Everything he said was true, and yet she didn't want to lose out on an opportunity that would never ever come again just because the timing sucked.

"You want forever, Dandelion." He touched her cheek and ran his thumb across her lower lip. "Getting engaged, planning for a baby proves that. I can't offer forever."

She looked at the angular planes of his face—austere masculine beauty. All man. All cowboy. The penultimate male as far as she was concerned, and Langston wasn't going to pass up on the chance to be with Bowen Ballantyne even if it was once or one week. This summer had dealt her pain, humiliation and loss. Why not kick off fall and a fresh start to her new life by making a few very pleasurable memories to warm her on the cooler, lonely nights coming her way?

"I'm not looking for forever, Bowen."

He raised his head, and the heat in his eyes seared her. "But—"

"Not now." She couldn't add *not with you* although she should have, but it would have been a lie.

She rocked up onto her knees so that she was level with him and closed the distance between them. She leaned in and traced her tongue around his lips. His mouth opened and he kissed her back until she was in his lap, her fingers tangled in the snaps of his shirt.

She kissed his tan neck and licked along the hollow of his throat. The light rasp of his five-o'clock shadow zapped nerve endings throughout her body.

"So…" She put a little distance between them, backing off and sitting on the ground tailor style again, facing him, their thighs touching. She moistened her lips hoping to look sexy but probably failing. She fought the urge to flip the hair she no longer had. Hating that she was so bad at this and that she lacked confidence, she kept her tone playful. "Tell me about this game you got going with Bodhi, and I'll let you know if I want to play."

CHAPTER NINE

"YOU'RE SO BEAUTIFUL." Bowen reached out to cup the smooth silk of her cheeks. His hands must be so rough against her delicate skin, but he couldn't help himself. She glowed with life, and he could still taste her in his mouth. "Ethereal."

Langston stilled. Apprehension clouded her gaze and a wariness he hated.

"But?" she asked coolly.

"I want to be with you." His fingers traced the straps of her pale pink tank.

Langston blinked and then braced herself. "But…" She let the word dangle there.

This was so hard. He didn't want to hurt her. Or anger her, or ruin the afternoon when she'd just found her way back into a saddle doing something she loved and was born to do.

"Even though I didn't recognize you immediately, I still remembered your eyes—the color, the way your soul shines through them, the millions of expressions that dance there. I always remembered your eyes." His voice was a gravel confession. "I was pleased to spot you the favor. I got the better deal." He played with one curl at her nape, which had escaped the rigid product she used, and he hated. He preferred her free and a little wild. "I wasn't going to ask for anything in return."

"Spit it out, Bowen," she said.

He could see her pulse kick up in her neck. He was dragging this out. Making it harder on them. "I haven't been completely honest with you." He smoothed his hands down her bare arms.

"You have a girlfriend!" She pushed at him and crab-walked away so fast that if it had been a rodeo event, she would have buckled.

"No, of course not." He was offended. "I would never ever cheat at anything, especially on a woman. Don't compare me to that jackass playing cowboy back at the Graff."

"OK. I'm sorry." Lang sat back down but didn't come closer. "You're just freaking me out a little." She reached for one of the water bottles filled with iced sweet tea, unscrewed the cap and took a deep drink.

Even the way she swallowed was sexy.

Damn, but he had it bad.

He sucked in a deep breath, took off his Stetson and ran his hands through his hair.

"You're right, but you're also wrong," he said, not wanting to continue.

"Bowen, if you weren't so dang tall, I'd turn you upside down and shake the words out of you."

"We are worried about Granddad," he said. "He intimated that he was thinking of selling the ranch."

Langston's pretty mouth moued as if to ask a question, but she didn't.

"We were all shocked. Worried. Not sure what was going on. The moms have wanted him to sell Three Trees and move to Denver so they could watch out for him. They don't want any part of the ranch. Never did, but we—all of us, me, Bodhi, Beck—can't imagine Granddad ever wanting to live anywhere else." All of his worry uncapped—the words now fizzing out under Lang's intense scrutiny.

"We all planned to live there. Work the land with Granddad until he wanted to retire. Keep the Ballantyne legacy alive. We figured we'd take care of Granddad on the ranch. Never thought he'd want to leave. He always said he'd only leave boots first."

Langston was quiet, clearly absorbing the information. She might not be as shocked as he and his cousins had been. Her daddy had walked away. Her two aunts. And then her granddad had sold up what was left of her legacy.

"Did you ask him why?"

"Every damn day. He avoids us. Says we'll talk after the Bash like that's some magical event that's going to make everything clear." He spun his hat around his hand. "I'm worried he's lonely. Tired of all the responsibility. Bodhi's worried about his health. Beck thinks he might need money, although Beck is drowning in drama of his own making, trying to get Ashni to take him back I think, although he won't talk about it."

Langston's hand was a whisper along his shoulder. She traced up and down his spine in a soothing rhythm. He shut his eyes, absorbing the feeling along with the warmth of the sun.

"And all the moms arrived Tuesday with a landscaping crew, a construction crew working on a few upgrades to the house and all of us have been working mostly up on Plum Hill on repairs to the big barn and the smaller one and also upgrades to the cabin and building an outdoor kitchen. I feel like we are all working so damn hard to just hand everything over to some rich stranger who will only visit a couple times a year. It's Ballantyne land. Ballantynes have lived and loved and fought and worked there for well over a century and a half."

He couldn't sit still any longer. He was on his feet pacing. The two horses looked at him curiously. Lang stretched out on the blanket, leaning back on her elbows, legs out, sun shining on her hair.

"I can't imagine Granddad anywhere but here, but maybe we're all being selfish, trying to hold on to something that no longer belongs to us," he confessed.

"It sounds like your mom and aunts are pretty serious," she said, her face creased in sympathy.

She had gone through this too, watching her legacy and her future get sold out from under her. Was he being a selfish jerk trying to explain what was going on in his life when Lang had so much on her plate? Probably, but the bitterness he was trying to keep at bay with his mother's arrival and her team that talked so easily about "upgrades" and a "more modern ranch profile that will appeal to buyers" just made him sick and angry.

"My mom will get some outrageous commission and whisk Granddad off to some condo in the city or assisted living facility where he'll be alone and wither, and I just can't believe in here—" he banged on his chest "—that this is truly what Granddad wants. I feel like the moms have just bullied him too long, and he's doing it to make them happy, but what about what makes him happy?"

Lang stood up and pressed her small body against his side, wrapping her arms around him. Her fingers drew circles on his lower back, and he had to resist relaxing back into her.

"Soooooo," Langston mused, "you're all worried about your granddad, but he won't talk about why he's changed his mind. What's the action plan Bodhi's sucked you all into? How do you think you can change his mind or get him to spill?"

Dang, she was quick.

"A Montana Rodeo Bride Game," Bowen announced sourly.

✪

"A WHAT?" LANG rocked back on her heels and stared at him a little wildly.

Bowen's mouth twisted without humor. "It's as crazy as it sounds," he admitted. "It was Bodhi's challenge. He thought that if one of us could get engaged—bring a potential bride to the Ballantyne Bash, it would get Granddad to see that his future is still on the ranch. He would feel the future of the next Ballantyne generation was assured."

"Why doesn't he feel that way?" Lang asked.

She was beginning to feel like Bowen wasn't going to answer. This man—so strong and appealing but so dang silent when she finally felt like they were making a breakthrough. Of course Bodhi would think of some way-out-there idea and turn it into a game. Mr. Flirt.

She tugged on his arm. "Let's eat," she said. "Tell me how the game works."

Lang sat down again, opened the small cooler and pulled out half of a sandwich, hoping it would help Bowen relax enough so that he could talk. Tension radiated off him like a force field.

"Going pro on the rodeo tour was something we all wanted—pitting our skills against each other and the best." Bowen took the sandwich she offered, unwrapped it and bit, chewing precisely. "We thought we'd do it two or three years and then settle on the ranch together," Bowen said. "But we started making good money, and the more we talked about it, we realized that for the ranch to support us, we'd need to make some serious investments in it, or have some side hustles to bring in extra income. We've all been living lean, saving, investing."

Bowen was so the opposite of everything her father was or had been. She hadn't spoken to him in years and didn't want to.

And why was she ruining a beautiful fantasy afternoon thinking about the past and her deadbeat dad?

"The Rodeo Bride Game," she reminded him, trying to not get off track with the movement of Bowen's strong jaw as he chewed. She was ridiculously crushing hard if she found a man chewing sexy. "You all just show up with a woman to the Ballantyne Bash, get down on bended knee, say some pretty words, she squeals and cries and Ben says, 'My boys.'"

"Guilty."

She laughed. "You boys have a lot of confidence in your appeal."

"Bodhi does," Bowen admitted. "It's not misplaced. It was his idea and then in some twist that always happens between the three of us, it became a game."

"Are you really going through with it, or is this going to be a long engagement or one that fizzles once you're back on the road?"

"No, it would be a temporary engagement just to get Granddad to halt the idea of selling the ranch and buy us some time to see what was wrong, what he's worried about."

"What are the other rules?" she asked.

Bowen took a deep swig of his tea, finally seeming to relax a little. "The woman has to be in on it, and it has to be a win-win."

"What's that mean?"

"The woman would be doing us a tremendous favor. We

wouldn't want her hurt. She should get something out of the deal."

That must have been Bowen's stipulation. She sat up, intrigued, a little pissed and also trying to ignore the pinch of hurt. She was done feeling like she was never enough.

"You're doing me a favor this week, so why didn't you ask me to be your rodeo bride for the game?" she demanded. "Asking me fits in with your rules."

The tension was back. Bowen stopped chewing and looked at her warily. "You had enough on your plate with Mason and the wedding this week and losing your baby," he said.

Langston felt something in her ease just a little. Bowen was so Bowen. Honest. Thinking of others before himself. And acknowledging her loss. Langston had felt she was the only one who grieved her baby.

"If I'm not a good choice—" Langston put down her sandwich; the few bites she'd already taken felt like rocks in her stomach "—who are you going to get to play?"

He didn't answer, his gaze focused on the valley with that long-range stare a person got when they see the destination they don't want to arrive at.

"I don't want you hurt. I don't want Granddad hurt. You'd be too real," he finally said. "We have a history. Your grandpa and mine were friends. Mine always watched out and had a soft spot for you. If I showed up with you, he'd believe it."

"Bowen Ballantyne." Langston gritted in pissed disbelief.

"Have you lost your dang mind? Isn't that the whole point—he believes the engagement?"

He closed his eyes. "Yes, but I don't want you hurt. Or him."

"What am I, one of those blown-out decorated Easter eggshells? I am not fragile or weak." Humiliation spiked. "You don't think I'm still crushing on you?"

Bowen held up his hand, placating, when Langston had long ago blown past being placated. "I'm done letting other people define my power." Langston made a fist and flexed her bicep. "I'm done letting other people tell me how I feel or thinking they know what's best for me. I'm taking back my life. My dreams. My power. I decide what I want to do. Not you or anyone."

"Fair enough," Bowen said soothingly like she was an edgy horse. "I didn't feel like I was doing that. You've always taken life by the horns, Dandelion."

"Funny." She narrowed her eyes at the nickname. "If it's one thing I have no intention of doing it's living my life being blown around in the wind."

"Hey now." Bowen's hands were warm on her arms, and as they soothed up and down her skin. It was all she could do to not close her eyes and lean into him. "Dandelions are one of my favorite flowers. Such pretty little bright yellow flowers, and then they shoot up and have this fluffy crown of glory just waiting for the wind's opportunity. The seeds travel on the wind, and the bit of fluff acts like a parachute to slow their descent. Did you know that the seeds can create a sort of vortex to keep themselves aloft? They can travel over half a mile or so just on one breath of a child."

Bowen's voice had always done something to her—turned her insides to strawberry jam. She used to try to irritate or challenge him just to get his attention and hear him speak. And to know that the hated childhood nickname that had so fussed her was something he liked…well.

"They are one of the few flowers found all over the world. They can take root and thrive in nearly any condition including cracked concrete."

OK then. She nearly told him then and there that he could call her Dandelion in private. And that scared her half to death.

"So Bodhi's playing with Nico," Langston attempted to get her stupid heart to calm down and close up again. "Beck's got Ashni." Why did they need to play since Beck had always had the same girlfriend? Oh. Dumb. Because they competed at everything. Always.

"Not unless he proposes for real. Ashni's been expecting a proposal for a while now. We aren't sure what's holding Beck back."

"Maybe this is just Bodhi's elaborate ruse to get Beck to finally cowboy up."

"No." Bowen shook his head. "I don't think so. Bodhi was just as shocked as all of us when Granddad said he was thinking of selling."

Bowen's blue-gray steady regard was addictive. She just wanted to throw herself into his orbit. Be his satellite. Same impulse as when she'd been a teen.

"Granddad threw us all off our game."

"And into a race to a proposal." Langston shook her head, smiling. It was so crazy and so Ballantyne to turn everything into a competition. A game.

"What happens if all of you propose?" Langston asked.

Bowen blew out a breath. "Honestly, even though it's a crazy idea, I can see it working," Bowen mused. "Granddad would feel like we were ready to enter the next stage of life. I was going to sit this one out, but it feels wrong to walk away. Not play. We've competed since we were little kids—me leading the way, Bodhi always trying to beat me, Beck determined to keep up and pass us both." He smiled but it didn't reach his beautiful eyes. "Even if we all propose, that too is a competition. The proposals are supposed to be public, maybe showy and done in front of Granddad and our moms."

"No pressure there."

To her surprise, Bowen smiled.

"The true win would be to ensure Granddad feels secure and happy in his future—on the ranch—if that is what he wants. He won't talk about why he's thinking of selling. We've all tried to reach him. Concocting this game idea is the first time Bodhi's engaged with us in a while." Bowen winced. "I've been worried about him all year," he admitted. "He's been reckless. Taking too many rank bulls and broncs. Riding wild."

"Definition of a rodeo cowboy."

"It's more than that," Bowen said, his voice heavy with sorrow and worry.

Langston covered his hand. "I'm sorry," she whispered.

"In a way, playing the game also makes me feel like I'm helping keep Bodhi grounded. Maybe it will kick Beck in the ass and get him to propose. He and Ashni are a good fit. Can't imagine them apart. And maybe Granddad does feel like there's no future on the ranch." He reached out and touched one of the tiny curls that fluttered around her face, and then traced his finger down her cheek and along her collarbone. His thumb rested against her pulse that kicked up in her neck.

He closed his eyes, and then his hand cupped her cheek. It was as if he were trying to rein in all of his emotions. She turned into his palm and kissed it, let her lips linger and trace his life line, his heart line, his fate line.

"It would feel like death to see it go." Bowen's voice was more of a broken growl. "My whole life Three Trees felt like home. We always planned to settle there. Retire from the tour together and each build a home over time. Work with Granddad and let him take steps back from the work when he was ready." He sighed. "We discussed living there even as kids. Looks like we may have left it too long. But I don't have to explain that to you. You lost your home."

"I didn't have a choice," she said softly. "But you do, Bowen. You can fight."

Langston rose up on her knees and straddled him. She felt his body leap in response, which made her bold. She feathered her lips over his and was thrilled by his intense response. It was like she'd lit him on fire. He pulled her tightly against his erection, and she gasped at the promise of his hard, straining length. Her lips parted, and his tongue thrust deep. He kissed her, heat and desire rising until she was breathless.

"We always have a choice, maybe not about the circumstances, but in how we react to what life throws at us. I choose to help you and help your granddad. I choose to play the Rodeo Bride Game."

"In that case—" he chased her lips with his and she leaned into his kiss "—you best come to supper tonight at the ranch."

Langston felt her heart soar, and for once she let it. Plenty of time to question her sanity later. "I always wanted to be in on one of your games," she confessed, not so subtly moving against him. She felt gratified when his breathing also fractured. "I like to play."

His eyes flared with heat as he caught her double meaning.

"Lang." He groaned and caught her hips and ground her against him, and she felt a rush of liquid heat pool low in her body. "Don't get hurt."

Okay, that was embarrassing. Was she that transparent?

"Worry about your own heart, cowboy." She flipped his hat off and pressed him hard into the ground before committing to a full-body kiss.

THE NEXT EVENING, Langston did a final walk-through of the ballroom and garden. She didn't need to consult her notes. They were the same notes and drawings that she'd made with Walker Wilder months ago for her own wedding. The garden and ballroom looked exquisite—she and the staff had worked most the morning to pull off the finished look. The rehearsal and lunch had gone smoothly. None of the anger or regret or hurt she'd expected to surface had.

Of course not. She'd moved on—all in on the rodeo bride dare or game or whatever Bowen wanted to call it.

"Just remember it's pretend," she muttered as she did a final perusal of her checklist on her tablet. The crew had gone home. The tables were set, beautiful, missing only the centerpieces from the Sweet Pea florist in Marietta, which would be delivered early tomorrow morning.

The room looked exquisite and ready for the film crew as well as for the wedding photographer. The spa day today had been a welcome and relaxing diversion for the wedding party as had the shopping trip in Marietta and Livingston yesterday. She'd only heard rave reviews about the catered dinner tonight at an elegant event center up toward the mountains. The wedding party had returned about half an hour ago. Some had headed into the bar, others to bed.

Langston took a few pictures for her professional portfolio and for the Graff's and then headed out to the garden to take a few more pictures. The moon was closer to full tonight. Maybe she would sit a spell and give herself permission to relive yesterday—it had been one of the best days in her life, and totally unexpected. The horse ride. The intimate conversation with Bowen where he shared his concerns. And then the family dinner at the ranch—Ben watching his three daughters chatting about the ranch updates and remembering their childhood. Bodhi hadn't left Nico's side, and Bowen hadn't left hers. Everyone had been interested in her job at the Graff—could it be permanent, would she stay on in Marietta, did she think she'd like to work with horses again? There had been so much warmth and energy. Love. It had felt like family.

She hadn't had that.

She hadn't realized how much she'd missed until last night. Her dinners with her granddad had been mostly silent—she'd sat at the farmhouse table alone doing homework, exhausted from school and chores and her grandfather had sat in the den watching the news or sports. Mason's family dinners had been more formal and not warm. The conversations had been more fact-based—business deals, accomplishments, financial information, events on their work or social calendar.

The family dinner at the ranch last night had been like a dream, a fantasy family dinner, something she would have seen in a movie. She'd loved every minute of it. She'd even agreed to help Bowen's moms and aunts with some of the prep work for the bash once the wedding was over tomorrow. She'd felt like she'd belonged—a feeling that had eluded her for all her life it seemed. But instead of making her sad at all she didn't have, it had filled her with determination. She wanted to have a family with that type of closeness and acceptance and love. She wouldn't again settle for less.

She heard a rustle behind her and spun around. Seeing Bowen standing there in Wranglers that molded to his thighs, a black T-shirt that fit him stupid hot, and a black Stetson angled low on his forehead jump-started her heart. He held a bag from Rosita's Mexican Restaurant that smelled delicious, but food—even authentic tasty family-owned Mexican—was not what she was hungry for.

"Bowen!" Like out of a movie he stood in the doorway between the French doors to the garden and the ballroom.

"I knew today was an all-day work marathon for you and figured you wouldn't get a chance to eat, so I picked up something before they closed."

She wanted to devour him far more than anything in the bag. Memories of their heated kisses at the ranch had heat rushing to her cheeks and other parts of her body. She still wasn't sure if she regretted Bowen stopping because he didn't have a condom or if she should be relieved. They were pretending. Playing a game. But yesterday kissing him and sitting beside him at dinner last night with his family had felt more real than anything else she could recall.

It was a bit like being the wrong actor in the right movie.

"Thank you." She felt warmed to her toes. "I'm pretty

much done until tomorrow morning," she said breathlessly. "The wedding is in the morning followed by a brunch, and then I'm heading out to the ranch to help your mom." Why was she talking? He knew all this. But her nerves were flying. Did she have the courage to invite him home? Would he say yes? Was she ready for that?

Ready or not, she knew she'd regret it to the end of her days if she didn't take the risk and go for what she wanted. She knew Bowen wasn't looking for anything permanent. And she probably wasn't ready for more, but opportunity was a fickle bitch.

"Thank you for bringing dinner, Bowen—" she stood on tiptoes to kiss him and savored his immediate warm response "—but I'm feeling more in the mood for dessert."

FOR THE FIRST time since she'd moved in with the bare essentials—she'd started selling or donating most of her things to prepare for her marriage and new home with Mason—the one-bedroom apartment felt homey. That was because Bowen was in it.

There had been an awkward pause at the door, and Langston feared Bowen would go all noble on her, saying he didn't want to hurt her and couldn't promise anything, but she was sick of not grabbing what she wanted. And she wanted Bowen. She always had. However long she could have him—one night or more.

It was time to stop hoping for crumbs. She'd been letting others define her—first as a defiant, mouthy, competitive kid desperate for attention, and then as she'd cautiously adulted—trying to fit in in college by acting less ranch and then pretzeling herself in Mason's mom's high-end corporate world. So now she was going to go for what she wanted.

Bowen shrugged out of his denim jacket and laid it carefully over one of the two hand-painted, restored dining room chairs from Brandel's Baubles, Fine Art and Collectibles, a local antique and restored treasures store that Langston loved to walk through and imagine how she would furnish the rooms of the house that she was even further away from being able to have.

"Do you really want me to make some coffee?" It had been her nervous blurt of an excuse to get him into the apartment when she'd feared he'd kiss her chastely at the door and disappear back into the night. This was so stupid. She'd been feeling so brave and daring, but now that he was here, in her space, she wanted him to make the first move. "Or do you want to take up where we left off yesterday afternoon?"

He prowled across the distance between them—not much, the apartment was small—but he moved like a man on the hunt, and her heartbeat jacked up to the roof of her mouth. This would never do. She wasn't sixteen anymore. Sheesh, she'd been bolder when she was a teen.

"Langston," he began, cupping her jaw. His thumb feathered across her raging pulse.

"Yes or no?"

"Yes," he said, but his eyes weren't saying yes, and he was way too tense, like he was waiting for something bad to happen.

She turned her back to him so he could unzip the black and white jumpsuit she'd worn today. She'd already kicked off her work shoes and peeled off her blazer. Hopefully one day she'd get better at seduction so the man would pounce, and she wouldn't have to shuffle through all this doubt.

"Langston." Bowen's hands were on her shoulders, and his mouth nuzzled her nape, but her zipper was untouched.

She leaned back into him, and her heart soared to feel the power of him straining at his jeans. Okay. She wasn't out of her mind or off base and every other analogy her anxious brain could dredge up. He wanted her, but he didn't want to hurt her. He was too kind for his own good. She could work with that.

"I know," she said, turning her head to kiss his hands. The memory of how they felt stroking her skin even as she'd been regretfully fully clothed was enough to send shivers through her body and peak her nipples.

Some woman someday was going to be the luckiest woman in Montana to finally snag his heart. He was a good man, all in caps. He'd come home after work not go bet and drink at sports bars or stink of perfume and lap dances from the strip club.

"I know you're heading back out on the road." She turned around so she could face him. "The rodeo is your life right now. Your career. I respect that. I admire that. I won't be waiting here for you. And I won't ever ask you to change. What we do tonight is just us enjoying each other with no ties, no expectations."

"You're okay with that?"

She'd expected him to sound relieved. Instead he seemed deeply skeptical and kinda pissed.

"Who's to say I won't break your heart, cowboy?" She played with his belt buckle.

"There is that," he said, his eyes darker, and heated, but he still wasn't jumping her.

Was Bowen Ballantyne going to judge her for finally not being a woman who went into every sexual encounter thinking that it meant something more?

"Men have casual sex all the time," she said—not that she needed to point that out to a top-tier rodeo cowboy on the pro tour. She'd seen the lines by the dressing room, by the rigs at the rodeo grounds, heard the whispered conversations at the bars and in the bathroom when the rodeo hit Missoula and Helena. "Women like sex just as much."

She sounded ridiculous. And pathetic trying to persuade him. Why did he have to be so damn honorable and cerebral?

"Bowen, I like you a lot." Did that sound too flip? Too weak? She ignored her massive understatement. "Heck, Bowen, why do you need to make this so hard? Jump off your high horse and roll around in the mud with me."

He looked a little shocked, and then a hint of a smile

touched his mouth. "Is that what you want, Dandelion, to get a little dirty?"

"A lot dirty. Filthy. With you."

Likely the worse seductive line ever, but he wasn't grabbing his jacket and ripping off the doorknob in his flight.

"We both want casual," she said sounding so reasonable she was proud. "I'm only in Marietta for the year. Then I'm out of here. I don't know where, but I don't want to stay in a town where everyone thinks they know me. I'm not looking for a man except for now—tonight, maybe the weekend if you're as good in bed as you look like you are."

Bowen choked back a laugh.

"I definitely need practice as this seduction game," she admitted.

"You're doing just fine, cowgirl."

"Not a cowgirl anymore."

"You'll always be a cowgirl, Dandelion. And a seductress." His voice was a deep rumble. He made a spinning motion with his finger. "Let me show off my zipper skills." His voice was graveled, and Langston's body was liquid with need.

She felt a little dizzy as she turned around and presented her back.

He kissed her nape, blew a little, kissed her again and whispered how beautiful she was, delicately made and strong as steel. The words and his touch created shivers that built from the pit of her stomach. He must have used his teeth, and Langston moaned as she felt and heard her zipper release inch by slow inch, and Bowen's hint of five-o'clock shadow teased her back.

The jumpsuit puddled at her feet, leaving Langston in her bra and underwear.

"Open your eyes, baby," he whispered.

Langston did, and gasped. She could see herself in the bathroom mirror across the length of the room. Bowen stood behind her, fully clothed, and she was in her underwear.

"Do you like to watch?"

"Bowen?" she asked shakily, not sure what he was asking, but she looked like a seductive, passionate stranger, flushed, the light from the one living room lamp a warm, orange glow lighting them both. Her lingerie was a pale, dusty rose color that looked almost nude in the mirror.

"Have you ever watched yourself come apart in a man's arms?"

"N-n-n-no."

"Do you want to?" Even as he asked her, he stood directly behind her, one wide, sun-browned hand spread out on her pale, flat stomach, and he rubbed his chin along her neck. She arched back into him, whimpering, wanting more. His other hand anchored at her hip.

Yes.

But her voice wouldn't work.

"I want to watch you watch me make you come."

It was the most decadent thing any man had ever said to her. She'd always wanted Bowen. She wanted to rediscover herself or reinvent herself into the woman she wanted to be.

This was jumping into that fire and beyond. Unrecognizable from anything she'd ever dreamed to do with Mason. The lights were on—dimmed, but on. She was nearly naked. He was fully clothed. They were standing. She wasn't even sure what he was going to do, but she couldn't wait to find out.

"Tell me what you want." One of his fingers played with the waistband of her bikini-cut panties, dipping below her panty line and stroking her sensitive skin.

"You," she whispered.

"How do you want me?"

Not a complicated question. She gripped his forearm to position his hand exactly where she wanted it. He was so close. Teasing her.

"Every way I can."

Langston trembled, waiting for what would come next.

"Touch your breasts." His voice was a soft growl in her ear that sent shivers coursing through her body.

"Like this?" She cupped the small mounds and then with her thumbs played with her nipples first through the stretchy lace and then dipping under.

"Exquisite." His approval cranked her heat higher.

One finger parted her slick folds and stroked her. "Keep watching," he bossed as her eyes drifted shut.

"Bowen," she moaned, feeling her legs tremble as he played with her sensitive nub, circling and pressing slow and then speeding up, until she could feel the pressure building. "Don't stop," she nearly wailed as she neared her crest but then he backed off.

"Lick your lips."

Langston did.

"Stroke yourself, show me how you like to be touched." He took her hand and guided it between her thighs.

She still wore her bra and panties, and Bowen reverently unhooked the front clasp of her bra and let it slide partially down her arms. Too passionate to experience embarrassment, Langston stroked herself, watching Bowen watch her in the mirror. It was the hottest thing she'd ever done.

As the pressure built, she approached that shimmering peak, but before she could crash over, Bowen threaded his fingers through hers and drew one of her fingers—slick with her juice—deep into his mouth. His tongue stroked along her finger much as she had been doing to herself.

She stared at his mouth. She was burning up. She was going to detonate.

"You taste like summer," he murmured and then he drew her hands back behind her back and secured them with her bra before she even realized what he intended.

"My turn," he told her and took over. Langston wasn't sure if she was even standing on her own. His fingers were magic, teasing her, stroking and then while his thumb worked its magic on her clit, he plunged two fingers deep inside her body and stroked her all the way through the most powerful orgasm of her life.

"Keep your eyes open or I stop."

She tried. She really tried. And as her body began to come down, he withdrew his fingers and traced a letter—B she thought—over her bared breasts.

"I want to touch you," she said shakily.

"After."

After what? The thought barely formed and then he picked her up, strode through her small apartment to her bed, laid her down and, still fully clothed, he spread out her thighs, jerked her bottom toward the edge of the bed and dropped to his knees, hooking her legs over his shoulders. Then his mouth was right where his fingers had been. Langston gripped the comforter to try to hold herself still as the burn and the physical sensations built.

She found herself chanting his name combined with "yes" and "more" even as she felt time tunneling so that she wasn't sure where she was or how long the sensual feast lasted. She clutched at him—her anchor in the storm he was creating. His body was so solid and strong when hers seemed to be flying apart, spinning, flying further and further away.

Finally, he was there, helping her scoot back on the bed although her limbs wouldn't coordinate at all.

"Shirt." She reached for him. "Naked." She'd been naked and thrashing, and he'd been fully clothed. She needed to touch him. She needed to drive him up and over like he'd done for her.

Bowen flashed a smile in the dim light percolating into the bedroom. His face was slick with her, and a primal satisfaction speared through her.

Mine.

"Fast." She pulled the snaps apart and Bowen shrugged

out of his shirt at the same time she heard his boots clunk to the floor.

Langston, propped up on her elbows, watched him, fascinated by his speed in shedding his clothes and the rigid bulge in his boxers. He pulled those off without hesitating and Langston hummed happily as he sprung free.

Bowen had already pulled a condom from his jeans pocket, and she held her hand out for it.

"If you didn't bring more, I bought some today," she said feeling bold and ripping open the wrapper with her teeth as if she'd done this most every day.

His eyes flared as she rolled the condom over his straining erection.

She thought he'd push her back down and thrust into her. She wanted that. To be covered, to feel his weight, to give him control. Instead he sat up, braced against the headboard and holding on to her hips, he pulled her onto his lap and impaled her inch by delicious inch.

"I've been imagining you riding me all week," he whispered in her ear, ceding all control.

Chapter Ten

Bowen stretched out on Langston's bed and listened as the shower turned off. He'd spent the night with her. Had fallen asleep next to her. Something he'd done with a woman maybe a handful of times. The night had been one, long sensual fest. He'd felt almost drugged as he lost himself in her body and her sensual responses to their lovemaking. Langston Carr was a very passionate woman. They'd made love twice and then they'd taken a shower, and he'd been unable to resist her again when she'd stroked and kissed and sucked him to a powerful climax with the hot water streaming down over both of them.

He wanted her again.

He got up. It wasn't even light. He hadn't figured she'd need to head into work this early, but with a late morning wedding and brunch at the hotel, there likely were a lot of last-minute details. He hoped he could be there with her for part of it to help stave off any lingering hurt. There must be some even though she claimed she'd moved on.

Or was he just grasping at excuses to see her?

Not that he needed any. She'd committed to the game, to helping his mom and aunts with the Ballantyne Bash. He hoped that meant she'd attend the steak dinner and dance with him, and then the Bash. But then what?

An unusual dread swirled in his gut. Last night hadn't felt like pretending or a game.

He needed to keep his head on straight just like when he competed or he'd be bucked off, stomped and left writhing in the arena dust, wondering what had just happened.

This was a rodeo hookup. It wasn't going to be more than that. But the stakes suddenly felt much higher. Bowen cursed himself because although he might not be the most savvy with personal relationships, even he knew that this could get out of control very quickly.

"Good morning." Langston came out of the bathroom, toweling off her hair. She smiled up at him, a little shy, and even as he'd been coaching himself that he should play it cool so that she didn't think this was more than it was—he doubted she had a lot of hookups—whereas that had been all he'd had. Immediately his actions belied his self-talk.

He wrapped his arms around her and pulled her into his body. He kissed the top of her head.

"I'm sorry I woke you."

"I wish you'd woken me up earlier." He nudged against her to show her what she did to him.

"Insatiable," she breathed, her voice catching with excitement. "Hold that thought until tonight."

He laughed, feeling lighter than he could remember and oddly reluctant to let her go. He took the towel and gently dried her off. He touched her hair as it stood out from her head.

"Cute." He smiled, thinking it made her look far more like a dandelion now than when Bodhi had created the name years ago. Still, he missed her long, wild curls.

"Ugh. I'm sorry. I have to hurry. I have to blow it dry and gel it into submission."

"Why?" he asked letting his fingers play now that it was silky again. Even damp, he could see the waves forming.

"Because it will just be a curly mass."

"I love the curly mass," he said. Then he tilted her chin up. "Why'd you cut it? Was it recently or…?"

She made a face. "I needed a reboot. I thought it would be more professional. And different from what I had last time I lived in Marietta," she said. "But really I was grieving losing my baby and the life I thought I was going to have." She blew out a breath. "As usual, I overreacted." She plucked at the cropped ends.

He cupped the back of her head and kissed her tenderly. "It's natural and healthy to grieve," he said. "There is no right way to do it. Let your hair curl if you want," he said. "It's you. Wild. Free. Beautiful."

He meant every word, but the impact—her deer-in-headlights look—was not what he was going for.

"I'm working at the ranch today and bringing my horse to the fairgrounds. But I'd like to see you tonight."

He didn't want to examine how his desire to see her had nothing to do with the favor he'd done for her, the ranch or the game.

She nodded, looking a bit shy. "You'll possibly see me sooner. Your mom asked me to come help with the party. She hired me through the Graff so there's no professional issues. The Graff is catering some of the food for the big bang Ballantyne Bash." She made jazz hand, star bursts on the six syllables.

He laughed. "Tell me she did not call it that."

"You know she did."

"So you'll be okay today?" he asked. "You don't want me to stop by the wedding—catch a dance with you?"

"Better than okay," she promised. "I do want to dance with you, but I'm on a team with a hot local cowboy playing a game that I believe involves dancing at the steak dinner on Saturday."

"Absolutely," he said, trying to ignore the pinch her lighthearted words caused in his chest. She was joking. Making light. That should relieve him.

Lang smiled a heart-stopping smile and then glanced in the mirror. She ruffled her hands through her hair and examined the effect.

"You are really asking for it," she muttered. "I think we're both going to be sorry about this."

"I won't," he said, not sure if he was talking about her not gelling her hair into submission or her jumping all into the Rodeo Bride Game with him.

✪

"LANGSTON, YOU GOT a minute?" Sheila poked her head out of the bridal dressing room. Her hair and makeup was done, but she was in her corset and slip, the bridal dress not yet slipped over her impressively detailed updo.

"Sure." Langston paused, her mind running over all the last-minute details. Everything was running smoothly. "What do you need?" she asked.

"Everything is fine," Sheila said, her face anxious.

"But…?" Langston prompted.

"This is going to sound weird, but…" Sheila looked down. "I wanted to thank you for being so cool about the wedding. The planning. My mom and Mason's mom were sure you were going to try to ruin it out of spite, but you didn't, and…and I'm not sure I would have been so forgiving."

Sheila's brown eyes beseeched her—nervous, guilty.

Forgiving? Had she been forgiving? That seemed too structured for how she felt.

"I don't know how I'm feeling, Sheila," Langston admitted. "What you and Mason did was a betrayal."

"I couldn't help it. He was so nice and exciting. I just fell for him so hard," she said eagerly. "And he said you guys were going to break up."

They'd been engaged. She'd been expecting his child. He had never once intimated that he wanted out of the relationship.

Langston opened her mouth and closed it again.

It really didn't matter. She didn't feel angry anymore. Or

hurt. She felt…relieved. And a dose of pity because even though Sheila got the baby and the lifestyle, she was also getting the man, and in Langston's opinion, a cheater was a cheater.

"Water under the Marietta Bridge," she said, realizing that she did mean it. "The arbor is set up. The justice of the peace has arrived. The musicians are warming up. Food, drink, everything's on schedule. You just need to relax, enjoy your day and be ready in about thirty minutes."

"Thanks, Langston." Sheila hugged her fast and hard and then stepped back. "Thank you. And…and I am sorry. I know it doesn't mean much, but I am." Sheila winced and then backed into the dressing room where her bridesmaids were laughing and likely already starting on the champagne, and firmly closed the door.

Langston did a last-minute check-in with the chef and kitchen staff and then her own staff. Despite the emotional drama, the event was ready and running on time. And her crew already had the rodeo decorations ready to go up in the lobby and front of the hotel once the wedding decorations were broken down.

The rest of this year is going to be even better, she promised herself. Bowen was an unexpected perk. Nothing more.

He can't be. He's heading back on tour next week.

She wished she could kick her inner buzzkill to the curb. She knew he was leaving. He'd made that clear. She'd agreed to the terms, so why not embrace the time they had and then happily wave goodbye, and if she could help Ben Ballantyne feel like there was still so much for the Ballantynes and their next generation, she'd take that as a win. Although the theory of playing a game with the cousins had been easier to stomach when she would just be there for the party. Now that she would be at the house for the next couple of days helping, there was a far bigger chance that she'd make a mistake. She'd never been a good liar.

She'd heard too many lies and broken promises from her dad. But she'd given her word to Bowen to help him out.

"There you are!" Mason's mom in a teal-blue suit dress startled her out of her reverie.

"Hello, Judith," she said, wishing her heart would settle. "I've checked in with…"

"Everything was fine. You have always planned and executed excellent events."

"So why'd I get fired?" Langston didn't want to be belligerent, but she was not going to get another opportunity to discuss this. Judith had abruptly fired her without a recommendation after years of work. It had been a professional, personal and financial hit.

"That's obvious," Judith said. "It would be awkward for Mason and his new bride and me to have you mooning around, but I must say you've rebounded magnificently—much more your lane."

Langston wanted to tell Judith exactly what she thought of the lane she drove in so imperiously, but Judith held out a stiff, ivory-colored envelope.

"We paid the bill with the hotel. I know it's not in keeping with the Graff to offer tips, but considering, I think you went above and beyond, and I didn't offer you a severance package before terminating you."

Langston wanted to toss the envelope back in her face, but why should she? She'd done nothing wrong. "I'd prefer a recommendation."

Langston wasn't even sure she wanted to stay in event planning. She'd stumbled into it, and she was good at it, but who knew what the future held?

Judith inclined her head. "I imagine," she said coolly. "I'll be honest. I was very leery about having you oversee the final days of the wedding for obvious reasons, so awkward for Mason, but his fault so..." She waved her hand. "I've emailed you a recommendation for your years of service that you can use after you get out of this no-stoplight town, and Mason has added a cashier's check for your earnest money on the townhouse, so we're all squared, yes?"

Were they? Langston was stunned by the turn of events.

"Mason had you sign the nondisclosure agreement." Her eyes narrowed. "It's legally binding."

"That agreement wasn't necessary." Langston channeled her best interpretation of a rodeo queen. Mason and his attorney had approached her this morning. It should have hurt, but it hadn't. One more sign that their breakup was for the best. "And thank you for this. We are, as you put it, most definitely squared away."

Langston turned on her heel and walked off—her heart soaring with possibilities. She'd told Bowen that there were always choices in life. She'd just been handed quite a few more.

✪

IT WAS FUN bossing Ballantynes around.

Langston had arrived at the Three Tree Ranch a little before three in the afternoon and she'd been sent out to Plum Hill to supervise setting up the dance area, a photo booth, and the casual country chic seating. Bodhi and Beck had been her help, and she had taken every advantage.

"Now you're just being mean, Dandelion," Bodhi had called out from on top of his ladder as he and Beck strung the lights inside the barn to give it a warm glow.

"Every time you use that stupid nickname, another strand of lights calls your name along with the silk floral arrangements you two goofs need to attach to hide the hooks."

"Goofs?" Bodhi countered. "Sexy cowboys, manly men, powerful..."

"Goofs." Langston wrapped another swath of burlap around the potted evergreen arrangements in the barn and anchored the material with a boldly patterned silk ribbon. "Seriously, Bodhi, you haven't matured since seventh grade."

"Ouch. I could show you how I've matured," he called down.

"No thanks. Don't want to go blind." She tossed two more silk floral arrangements at him, which he caught. He held one in his teeth while he tied the other one down.

Langston snapped a picture of Bodhi at the same time Beck did.

"Jinx," she sang out.

"You are not posting that."

"I so am. And tagging you and the pro rodeo tour. I can hear the hearts breaking all across the US."

"Does Bowen know what he's getting into?" Bodhi peered down at her.

"A tornado and class 4 hurricane? Yeah, he can't wait."

"He always was a masochist."

"Nope. Genius with impeccable taste."

Beck snorted and Bodhi laughed. "Look at her defending her man," Bodhi said.

"Is Bowen your man?" Beck wobbled on the rafter and Langston stopped wrapping the evergreens in burlap in case she had to break Beck's fall, which would likely kill them both.

"Have a care, Beck."

"You do know what I do for a living, right?" Beck dismissed her fears. "But back to Bowen. I know you had it bad for him—"

"Forever and ever," she interrupted Beck's trip down memory lane. She hated how she felt a little pang. She wasn't looking for forever now, but the game and playful teasing with his cousins was easy and seductive and wove such a warm feeling of fun, belonging and camaraderie that she was worried she'd get beaten by her own game.

When she'd arrived, Bowen was heading out to get bales of hay for guests to sit on—apparently they didn't have the right kind at the ranch because all of theirs were for the livestock over the winter. He'd stopped, crooked his finger at her, and breathlessly she'd run across the front yard from where she'd been catching up with Ben Ballantyne and all three of his daughters.

"Don't be shy," Bowen had said. "No kiss for your man? You had no problem jumping on my runner in the past."

She'd tried to stomp down her pleasure at the "your man," bit, but she jumped into her role as starstruck girlfriend. She'd jogged toward Bowen's truck and jumped up and kissed him. She'd expected a brush of his lips. Not a kiss that ignited her whole body.

Then he'd played with the curls that kinked all over her head and smiled. "Love these," he said. "I could play all night with these and other curls."

She'd flushed furiously and dug deep for some sort of sophisticated polish.

"Maybe I'll let you," she said, a bit embarrassed she'd changed her wild-hair-curbing routine for Bowen Ballantyne, but honestly, what woman wouldn't give him what he wanted?

Four pair of eyes had silently grilled her when she'd returned for what Ben Ballantyne had called "the girls' marching orders." It was one thing to try to deceive her former fiancé and his family that she'd moved on and couldn't care less and in the process realize that she truly did no longer care. But it was quite another to lie to people she had known and admired for much of her life.

And to see Ben Ballantyne's face light up. "Boy finally found a lick of sense," Ben had said and then, still smiling, he'd headed out to meet up with his foreman. She'd felt guilty over that. He'd truly seemed pleased. And Bowen's mother? The piercing look she'd shot Langston hadn't been half as intense as the look from Bodhi's mom.

So now she was taking out her discomfort with the Rodeo Bride Game on the two victims she'd been assigned.

"You bought your tux yet for your wedding?" She yanked Bodhi's chain a little harder.

"Already had the measurements, and the tailor is making the final adjustments—I need a longer inseam." She could see his smirk from way down on the ground while he balanced in the vaulted ceiling on a cross-section of beams.

"For your ego." She rolled her eyes, and tried for the fourth or fifth time in the past hour to not ask Bodhi why he had a few faint bruises coming up on the side of his face. She suspected he'd been in a fight, especially as Beck surreptitiously watched Bodhi like he was worried about him. But the Ballantynes were so close—competitive but close.

"Ouch. What are you going to wear to the party, Dandy, something unconventional or a traditional white gown? I picture you in a—"

"Don't say anything." She tossed another silk bouquet his way. "I planned to wear white, but then I gave my wedding gown to a women's organization that donates clothing to women trying to re-enter the workforce or women needing clothing for special occasions, so Bowen and I decided that we are going in Halloween costumes. I can't decide between him being a hotdog and me mustard or him a glass of Coke and me a straw."

Bodhi laughed so hard he lay across the beam jiggling as he tried to gasp in air.

Langston tossed the last two bouquets to Beck to fix in place.

"My work here is done, boys."

"Please, please, go for the mustard. I want to see the moms' faces. I need to see that before I die."

"Plenty of time for mustard visions, Bodhi," Lang said. "We're all stuck with you for decades more."

She expected a snappy comeback and was surprised when he stopped laughing, straightened, and he didn't flip her any manure back. Dread trickled down her spine. Was he embarrassed for her that she'd insinuated that she'd be in his life for years? She was relieved when she heard a truck.

"Bowen's back. Time to stop pretending you're both monkeys in the circus and come back to earth like mortals. We need to get the bales of hay arranged. The truck with the tables and chairs and stage should be arriving in…" she looked at her Apple watch "…twenty minutes."

"No break, boss?" Beck called out.

"Not for the wicked."

"Bodhi, keep working," Beck said as Bodhi began to climb down.

"Or the weary," she added, "and I'm looking at you, Beck."

The rest of the afternoon passed with friendly smack talk as the four of them were joined by Nico and Ben Ballantyne and a crew to set up the stage and sound system as well as arrange the rest of the seating and décor for the barn and the surrounding area.

Bodhi and Nico tied down the cushions on the chairs and the tablecloths on the scattered arrangement of slightly more formal seating for those who wanted to eat at a table, while Bowen and Langston put slip covers over the bales of hay.

"These are nice," she commented.

"My grandma made them, and each year I pull them out and wash them, and then at the end of the party, I collect them and wash them and fold them back up and seal them until next year."

"It's a cool idea," she said touched that Bowen took such care with his grandmother's slip covers.

"Glad you like them since we have dozens to put on."

Bodhi and Nico left to set up the photo booth, and Beck muttered an excuse that he was going to meet Ashni at the end of her art class she'd taught at Harry's House this week.

He took off, barely hiding his eagerness, but did offer his granddad a ride back to the main house.

"Alone," Bowen murmured in her ear as she bent over a hay bale to slip the cover on. "Finally. The whole time we were doing this, all I could think about was how much I wanted to kiss you wet and senseless and take you hard on one of these."

Langston's heart nearly jumped out of her chest.

"What about—?"

"You really think Bodhi and Nico are going to set up some silly costumes and props for the photo booth and rush back here for another job on the list?"

"That doesn't sound very pretend to me," she said and immediately wished she hadn't because all day she had been thinking about Bowen and what they'd done together, how much more she wanted to do, and none of it felt pretend.

"Are you up for making new memories?"

"Yes." She tried to keep her voice strong and not breathless.

"Show me," he said.

Smiling, and feeling a little daring, Langston cued her phone to the Bluetooth speaker set, and flipped on the lights to test them. It was still afternoon so sunlight streamed in the wide-open doors, but the golden lights strung throughout the structure looked so pretty.

"Sound and lighting check," she said. "And now a full equipment check." Her gaze drifted down to the growing and thrilling bulge in his Wranglers. "It's important that we are very thorough." She hooked her leg up and around Bowen's waist and he pulled her up to him. She pulled open the snaps of his shirt even as he peeled off her T-shirt so that they were skin to skin before they sealed their lips together.

"I plan to be very, very thorough," he murmured against her mouth, his hands already cupping her breasts.

CHAPTER ELEVEN

SATURDAY AFTERNOON, BOWEN had watched Beck keep his seat on a thrashing bronc that seemed to spin as much as buck. His cousin would enter the finals tomorrow as the competitor to beat in that event. Bodhi had done a masterful job riding in the saddleless bronc, but later during his bull-riding event he'd had a slight miscalculation with his dismount, ending up injuring his hold-hand wrist.

Of course Bodhi wouldn't go for an X-ray. He was "fi-ne." His brace had taken most of the impact—Bowen hadn't even known Bodhi had been wearing a brace. He hadn't been able to get too involved in changing Bodhi's mind because he was riding toward the end of the lineup.

Most of the riders were hitting the dirt.

"Ouch, makes you think bull riders are some kind of cra-zy," Bodhi said as another cowboy was flung off within a couple of seconds.

"Something like that," Beck said. He'd been watching from the stands with Ashni and some family friends but had hurried backstage to check on Bodhi.

Bowen looked at his cousins—Beck standing quiet and worried next to Bodhi, who was running his mouth in commentary like he was auditioning for an announcer role, which, come to think of it, he'd be really good at. The whole time Bodhi had his arm slung casually around Nico's shoulders looking so much like a real couple that Bowen felt a stab of unexpected envy. Bodhi made it look so easy to play the game, but Bowen had to keep reminding himself that Lang was temporary. Not his to claim.

And why was he thinking like this?

He'd set the rules. She'd just agreed.

He unobtrusively flexed his right hand. It still ached bone-deep from its clumsy encounter with the hammer on Monday. He'd felt it had been a deep bruise, but it still hurt, and working flat-out on the ranch this week hadn't given him any rest. Maybe he should have been wearing a brace or heading off for an X-ray.

Of course Bodhi noticed.

"You good?"

"Better than." His stern tone brooked no follow-up questions. Not that anything or anyone could shut Bodhi down.

"I can wrap it for you."

"I got it." Bowen turned to get some more medical tape from his kit.

"Heads-up." Bodhi pulled some tape out of his pocket and tossed it at him.

He quickly wrapped his hand tighter than usual but loose enough to keep the circulation free. Beck stepped in and helped. Bowen felt himself relax. He loved this part of the rodeo. Family. Competing but always being there for each other. Sure, lately he'd often thought about stopping, returning home, but he'd be lying if he said he wouldn't miss the competition, pitting his skills against so many others.

He'd also miss being with Beck and Bodhi. He'd always figured they'd be at the ranch together with Granddad. Building new memories. New lives. But what would he do if he didn't have the ranch to come home to and steward? Sure he'd had some luck selling a handful of country songs to a song producer, Rich Steven's Armadillo Dreams Music, but that wasn't a solid career plan. Even adding in occasional open mic nights wasn't a business strategy without the ranch. Music likely wouldn't support him. It was a hobby not a job. Music wouldn't help him support a family.

Family?

Where had that thought come in? That was the problem with games. He'd start playing, and he'd play to win.

He hadn't been able to get his mind off Langston. They'd made love on a hay bale in the barn where there was going to be music and dancing on Sunday night. What was wrong with him? He wasn't spontaneous. And then they'd gone back to her place to lose themselves in each other all over again.

How was he going to drive away next week like nothing had happened?

That was the deal.

Bodhi did it all the time.

Would he this time? Bowen hadn't seen Bodhi without Nico for most of the week. Could he finally be serious?

Bowen couldn't imagine, but if he were, would he be able to sway Granddad? Would Beck finally propose to Ashni? Was it possible that the Rodeo Bride Game could improbably work?

And what about me?

Bowen gave himself a stern mental kick to regain his focus.

And then he was up. Beck helped him with the flank strap and weighed in on the bull's attitude. Bowen watched the bull, restless and irritable in the pen. It was going to be a good ride, a high-scoring bull—if he could keep his seat. If his hold hand held. If it didn't, he was out for the weekend. He'd entered only bull riding this time, hoping to save his body for the next five weeks of the tour.

Every time he climbed on a bull could be the last time. Every cowboy knew that, but every cowboy had to think going in that he was absolutely going to stick the ride. Couldn't overthink it. Let the adrenaline, body and muscle memory do the work, but as Bowen climbed on top of the chute, timing the way he'd drop down and brushing his boot across the bull's back so he knew he was coming on board, he risked a look into the crowd.

Too many people to just spot one, but he thought he caught a glimpse of platinum curls off to the side of the grandstands. The woman was partially blocked by a thin, serious-looking cowboy in a black Stetson. Was that her? Was she watching? She'd promised. He'd never had a woman in the stands just for him. A ribbon of hope unfurled in his soul as he dropped down, tucked his boots back and angled his body up nearly on his hold hand and wrapped and rewrapped his grip. He angled up and a little forward toward the bull's massive shoulders.

No time better. Bowen gave the nod and the chute slid open. Bowen and the bull as one hurdled into the arena.

LANGSTON HAD MADE it back to the rodeo later than she'd anticipated. She'd skipped the parade and speeches and opening ceremonies. She knew exactly when the barrel racing started. She didn't know the competitors. The horses. Not anymore. That life was over. She'd made peace with it.

Except after spending time with Bowen, she felt Marietta and horses and ranch life seeping back through her pores down to her bones. Her past no longer felt so distant or forgotten. She'd loved the ride with Bowen on Wednesday afternoon. And working at the ranch yesterday had felt so right. How could Ben Ballantyne even entertain the thought of selling for a moment more?

Maybe Bowen was right. He didn't want to. His daughters did—although all three of them hadn't been afraid to get their hands dirty jumping in with the landscapers and jumping in on the projects at the main house. Last night while they'd been preparing a late, light dinner, Bowen had shaken his head as his mom and her sisters had all headed up to the attic in "work clothes" that consisted of designer jeans and cashmere tanks and cardigan twin sets. They all had hands full of trash bags intending to "clean, organize and toss generations of trash."

Langston's heart had thumped in alarm. It had seemed like the moms really did intend to prepare the ranch for sale.

"Does it worry you?" Langston had asked as she'd cut some late summer squash and peppers to make veggie kebobs for the grill along with the steak Bowen had marinated.

He hadn't answered, but he'd seemed amused when the moms had trooped back downstairs five minutes later, astonished that the attic had been mostly cleaned out and important mementoes had been toted and labeled already.

"What do you think we do when we come here?" Bowen had lightly chastised his mom. "We work—ranch work, repairs, cleaning out barns, sheds, the house. Whatever Granddad needs done, we do. Whatever he needs, we'll find a way to get it for him."

"Anything?" his mom had challenged arching a carefully crafted brow.

"Anything," Bowen had replied, clearly a challenge.

The air had felt electric, and Langston had racked her brain for a way to neutrally intervene and redirect the energy and emotions. She was supposedly good at this. Being an event planner meant that she dealt with so many different people often in what should be fun but could become stressful situations.

"How about a pre-dinner cocktail out on the back porch?" Langston had suggested. "Nico, Bodhi's…" She'd hesitated over the word *girlfriend*, which was dumb because that was the whole point of the happy families thing they were doing here, but it had felt like a lie, and Langston had always wanted to live honestly—even though she and Bowen had jumped into the game more than a little enthusiastically. Not that Nico and Bodhi seemed to be acting, and if they were, they were dang good at it and should strongly consider changing careers. "Nico drove to Bozeman to order wine for the party, and she brought back several bottles for us to sample."

The moms had liked that idea and had grabbed a corkscrew, glasses and the wine, and headed out to the back patio.

"My girl is brilliant." Bowen had pulled her to his side.

His girl. The words found a place in her heart too easily, fit too snugly, and she had to make light of it, but it had been hard with the way his eyes had sparkled so warmly at her.

Mason had never seemed to be especially pleased by something she'd done. Never. And then Bowen had kissed her, and she'd forgotten about the veggie kebobs, the salad she was making, the corn she was shucking until a quiet clearing of a throat had startled them apart. Ben Ballantyne had stood in the kitchen, and Langston had forgotten how to breathe.

She flushed, imagining that he could hear her slamming heart from across the room.

"Just getting some ice for the beer and another wine,"

Ben said walking over to the large Sub-Zero freezer. "Maybe you'd like a bit too." Ben had looked pointedly at Bowen, who'd looked a bit like a boy getting his hand caught in the proverbial cookie jar.

The point was to look like a couple happily headed toward engagement, but Langston had felt guilty and Bowen had seemed embarrassed, going so far as to whisper "sorry" to her when he had resumed preparing the steaks and she had started back on finishing up the kebobs and salad.

What part exactly had he been sorry for? Kissing her? Dragging her into his family drama and the game? Getting caught? All of it had made her feel more alone.

Langston looked into the crowded rodeo stands, trying to shake off yesterday's memories. Her emotions were all over the place, and she needed to get herself under control. She and Bowen were playing a game. Having fun. She shouldn't have feelings to sort out.

Bowen was out of her league—too everything. Too masculine, too sexy, too cowboy appealing and too many things to name: strong, confident, kind, intriguing. She was going to run the risk of falling too hard if she didn't catch herself now.

She decided to watch the bull riding from the side of the grandstands. Sitting with Bowen's family would be too much like being a part of his world, and in a few days she would be nothing to him but a pleasant memory. She could see without blocking anyone and make a quick exit. No playing the public girlfriend full of pride for her man while she sat with his family cheering him on.

The lie was wearing on her, confusing her, and she needed to protect herself.

Langston leaned against the fencing, mercifully in a bit of shade from the grandstands and watched cowboy after cowboy hit the dirt. Between the Telford and the Wilder bulls, the cowboys were not having a good day of it. She gnawed on her lip as another bull rider's name was called.

"Hello, Langston," a low voice said quietly next to her.

She knew that voice, but her brain wouldn't compute for a moment. She stared straight ahead and watched the rider and bull come charging out of the gate, much like her heart felt like it was doing—ready to jump and spin and burst out of her chest and make a break for freedom.

Papa.

Like she was still a nine-year-old girl begging him to stay, again and again, but he'd just keep leaving. And when he came home, it had never been for her.

"Been a while," he said.

The bull rider rolled to the side and under the bull at the three-second mark. The rodeo clowns raced in to distract the bull, which got in one solid kick to the rider's protective vest before bucking off in a short triumphant trot around the arena before heading back to the chute.

Not long enough.

"About sixteen years," she said, still not daring to look at him.

"Thought it was about that."

Half her life. How much time had he actually been present if she combined all the visits home that had been more about finding a place to crash and cadge money from family or friends before heading out on the next exploit than it had been about seeing her? One year, maybe less?

She stiffened against the fence. Had he somehow learned that she had been given a severance check and her earnest money back?

That's too suspicious and paranoid even for you.

Was it?

"Why you here now?" she asked and finally turned toward him, bracing herself for what, she didn't know.

Long, thick hair fell in waves past his shoulders. He had a wiry frame, a bit too thin, hawk-like features and deep blue eyes that looked almost black. He looked good. Way too good for how she'd imagined him all these years: drinking, gambling, womanizing, telling stories that got bigger with each telling.

"The ranch was gone a long time back. Buttercup's gone. My home is gone. Money's gone. Grandpa's gone. My mom is gone. All of it, everything is gone."

God, she wanted to hit herself. Yell to make herself shut up. Dandelion Carr, no mama or daddy, just a bitter, tired, disappointed old man taking care of her. Wild child. No one to take her in hand. No one to care. Pity. She'd had a lot of that growing up. And a wariness like she was a feral cat that would maybe claw and bite.

She wasn't that sad, lost girl anymore.

She was a woman. Strong. In charge of her life.

She notched her jaw and glared at him. She wouldn't give him a penny of what she had. Not even if he were dying—which he probably wasn't but would lie about without blinking and not feel a pang of guilt. She wouldn't even pay him to go away. Everything she had she'd earned the hard way. And she was keeping it.

"You took it all," she said coldly. "There's nothing left for you and everything I have is mine. I built it through hard work."

She turned her attention back to the arena, her breath coming in puffs. She wanted to storm off like this was a movie shoot, and he'd delivered the line to cue her escape.

"I figured you'd see it that way," he said neutrally.

"There is no other way to see it."

"Two sides to every story."

"And you are a champion storyteller." She breathed through her hurt, amazed she could still speak as her chest felt constricted like a squeezed sponge. "Don't bother. I don't want to hear it. I grew out of the wanting a bedtime story two decades ago—probably because I never got any." She turned back, hoping to char him with another hot glare.

She saw him swallow hard, and a shadow skittered across his face.

Good. She wanted to score against him. The strength of her anger scared her. She was beyond all this. She'd moved on. Let go of the pasts—Marietta and Mason. *Don't count the losses. Focus on the goals and the gains.* That had been her mantra for so long.

And yet here she was in Marietta. A little girl again. Raw. Wanting to strike at someone, something. And there was no horse to mount up and ride away from her demons. No Buttercup to train to be faster, corner sharper, win so she could show everyone that she was a champion even though no one else cared but her.

Bodhi's name was called. She heard the man who was her biological father—not her papa—suck in a breath and take a half step forward, his eyes fixed on the chute.

She too watched intently. So much could go wrong in eight seconds—much more than could go right.

The music. The announcer. Langston could barely take it in. Stories and stats about Bodhi—the announcers always took a bit more time with the hometown cowboys. She should take this time to leave. But she'd come to see Bowen, and she wasn't going to let anyone or anything scare her off. She could see Bodhi on the top of the chute, talking to Beck. They were clearly conferring. Then Bodhi dropped down. Langston felt her palms dampen. She hadn't been to a rodeo in so long. She'd been too afraid it would kick up too many memories.

And here was one of her biggest, darkest memories beside her.

"Walk out and meet your every fear past the halfway mark," she mumbled, the words dredged up involuntarily.

She felt her father's quick scrutiny.

"You remember that?"

Had her father said that? What a joke! He'd run from everything hard his entire life—debts, child-rearing, manning up to nothing and leaving all the hard work and cleanup to others.

The chute released and Bodhi and bull came charging out the gate. The bull bucked down, reared back and spun in a fierce balletic move, and Bodhi countered each move seemingly effortlessly. Sometimes it seemed as if bull riders were clinging to the bull—trying to muscle through the eight seconds with a combination of fear and stubborn determination. Bodhi seemed to be riding the bull like it was just a fun afternoon hanging out with his friends and family and showing off a bit. He appeared to be floating above the thrashing animal athlete a little almost as if he were controlling the moves. She'd never seen anything like it.

The bell and light went off, making Bodhi the first bull rider to stick the eight seconds. The crowd went electric, jumping to their feet and cheering and waving hats and Copper Mountain rodeo bandannas. Something was off with his dismount, and for a moment it looked like his hand took a hard hit from the bull's head, but he pulled free and made it up and over the fence.

"He has a gift," her bio dad stated.

"Bowen's better," she said quickly, feeling a rush of pride and ownership that she had no right to claim.

She crossed her arms and stared at the chute, willing Bowen's name to be called so she could get out of here. Get away from the awkward reunion she'd never wanted. Get away from the scrutiny of a small town that might notice the father-daughter reunion even though they'd both left the town years ago.

But she'd told Bowen she'd watch him, and she was not one who ran away when things got tough, like the man beside her.

Why was he here?

It was strange. He was so different than how she remembered. He seemed smaller, more contained. Not surprising—she'd been a child, desperate for him to notice her, to love her, to be proud of her.

"Why are you here?" she demanded unable like always to keep quiet and non-confrontational.

He sighed, one that seemed to dredge something out of his very soul, and despite not wanting to, Langston looked at him again.

"I was a crap dad," he said.

She wanted to say something sarcastic—understatement of the century. And no she wasn't going to try to talk him out of that assessment, but his gaze was so steady and direct, his expression so somber, that even though he looked amazingly like she remembered him, he seemed more tragic, as if something had sucked the magic, the life force out of him. She remembered how she'd been so proud of her daddy. He'd always seemed so much more alive than anyone else. Lit from within. Bathed in fire.

"Crap son. Crap partner. Crap man," he said.

Somehow hearing his admissions got harder—like staring

too long into the sun. Her eyes burned and she turned back to the arena as rider after rider shot out of the chute. Two more riders hit the dirt. Three had made it to the finals tomorrow along with Bodhi so far.

"I'm not going to disagree. Why tell me something I've always known?" She was not going to forgive him. She wasn't. Not ever. She hugged that truth close.

"I got sober eight years ago."

"Eight years!" She pinched her lips shut. She would not engage. Eight years. She'd been in college struggling to stay there—working nearly full time so that she could pay her tuition, books and supplies, her housing, feed herself and keep her car running so she could make it to her classes and her two jobs.

Her grandpa had sold the last of his ranch.

And he'd been sober. Free and clear to do what he wanted. Not a care for anyone in the world but himself.

Sober. Wasn't he supposed to atone to all those he'd hurt? Why not do it when she would have given a shit? When it would have made a difference?

"I tried before then, but it took a couple times to take for good. I got free of the gambling addiction earlier. The juice had a harder hold."

She felt her whole body recoil. The juice. Like it was the alcohol's fault he'd been so self-centered, weak and selfish. But, still, getting sober was hard. And it was probably the reason why he was still alive. She should at least acknowledge that though she didn't want to admire anything about him.

Bowen's name was announced. She stepped closer to the arena so her biological father was no longer in her peripheral vision. He was in her past. She wanted him to stay there. She needed him to stay there.

But even as she stood holding her breath waiting for Bowen to charge out of the chute into the arena, she knew Bowen wasn't her future. She knew that, but she didn't care. The kick in her gut told her that it was already too late. Her heart had blasted way past becoming emotionally involved.

The chorus from Aerosmith's "Sweet Emotion" blared over the speakers and then the chute released, and Bowen flew out of the gate. Her breath clutched her throat, and her fists balled up to her cheeks. She stared, terrified to miss anything. How did he stay on? The bull seemed more massive, more riled, more fiercely determined than any of the others to toss off its arrogant rider.

But Bowen hung on, fluid, moving in counterpoint with the bull like he could read its moves. He was like a dancer, swaying with the bull like ballet partners. Tears welled in her eyes. He was so beautiful.

And he's mine.

He'd been inside her yesterday afternoon on a hay bale and later in her bed. And that amazing man who was all about family and responsibility and helping out when he was needed was going to be hers tonight. And tomorrow. And she didn't want to miss a millisecond of her time with him by being afraid that she would get hurt.

Pain was a given. She'd learned that a long time ago.

Bowen dismounted. Waved to the crowd. She whistled and jumped up and down screaming his name and wishing she'd made her way up into the stands and squeezed in somewhere. She'd always been able to make a place for herself. Maybe he'd have been able to see her if she'd done that.

But she could go to him now. He'd given her a pass to get backstage. She could stay with him. Not miss a moment of their time together.

She turned back to her father. Even to think that word sounded so foreign. She'd outgrown the need to have a father a long time ago.

"Why come now?" she demanded, the adrenaline from the shock of seeing him merging with the adrenaline and surging emotions of watching Bowen ride. That she knew she'd lose Bowen like she'd lost everyone else made her edgy and hostile.

"Is this a sober thing? You want me to absolve you? Forgive you for never being there? For drinking and gambling away our birthrights and leaving your father with nothing but broken dreams and enough money to limp off to another state where he still had a handful of friends? You want me to say it's okay that you left your only child—that I know of—without a home or family or my college scholarship because my horse could fetch more money than a lot of the broken-down equipment on the ranch?"

By this time, Langston was up in his face, and she didn't care. She had no interest in playing nice.

"You want congrats that you're sober and free of addiction? Fine. Great. Congrats. Glad you're alive. Hope you stay healthy. But that's it. You are not forgiven. You will never be forgiven. You're not part of my life."

She turned to leave.

"Your granddad forgave me," he said softly. "We're talking again."

She closed her eyes. Of course he'd loved his only son more than anything else in the world—including his two daughters and his granddaughters.

Was that what she and her granddad had in common—loving someone who couldn't or wouldn't love you back?

What to say? Nothing. Langston kept walking and to her supreme shock, he did too.

"I don't want to talk to you."

"I get that, so listen."

She didn't want to listen, but she could hardly run away with fans starting to descend from the bleachers. There was only one way to the backstage area, and of course that was choked with families and sponsors.

"I know I fucked up, Langston. I can't change that. But I want to build a relationship with you," he said, stunning her. She halted as a few people bumped into her. "I know that's up to you. And I know it won't be easy."

No. It would be impossible. And her bio dad didn't do difficult, not with people.

"I want you to know that I accept it will take a lot of time and effort on my part to try to build a bridge between us. I accept that you still may want nothing to do with me. But I will make the effort. Again and again. I'm here for the long haul, Rocket."

Rocket. She'd forgotten he used to call her that.

She stared beyond him, over the heads of the people milling about and the sign that said backstage passes required.

"I have a job as a stock contractor for the Montana rodeo circuit. I've been working with them for a few years now. I've bought some land in the foothills of Copper Mountain. I built a house—most of it on my own."

She stared at him, feeling so furious and bewildered and confused by her reaction and the emotions clawing at her heart. She didn't care about him or his house or his sobriety. So why did she feel like she'd swallowed a blender and he'd hit the on switch?

"I'm moving back to Marietta. It's my home base. I wanted to tell you."

What he chose to do had nothing to do with her. Nothing.

Why was he so blurry?

"There's a room for you there if you ever need it. You have a home again if you ever need it." His voice was soft, insistent, persistent, unlike anything she remembered from his joy-filled, boisterous shout-outs from her childhood.

Langston turned and ran for the narrow gate, pulling the pass out of the back pocket of her jeans and waving it wildly as she squeezed through groups of milling people to finally make it past the guard and out of the sun and the noise and the jumble of too many conflicting emotions.

She looked around, feeling almost wild with the need to find Bowen. To absorb his quiet strength and calm in the face of everything raging inside of her.

It wasn't fair, she knew that, but finding Bowen seemed like survival and she was operating on instinct now.

She spotted him talking with Beck and Bodhi and his granddad. She pulled up short, breathless. He turned and saw her, and she froze. Did he really want her here? Was she interrupting? Should she…?

"Hey, baby, you made it," he called out, the smile and welcome in his voice as much as in his expression. He headed toward her at a jog, and something foreign inside of her burst open and gushed out.

He looked so solid and beautiful with his protective vest dark and tight against his body and his black and brown chaps hugged his thighs reminding her of how he felt cradled by her body.

She ran and threw herself into his arms.

"That was an amazing ride. The best. No one's done it better." She rushed the words even as her eyes burned and her chest compressed. She clung to him like a monkey even with some of his family there. And then to her complete shock and humiliation, she burst into tears.

Chapter Twelve

"Hey." He held her close, and she hid her face into his neck. "Easy now. What happened?" He tried to keep the surprise out of his voice as his hand smoothed down her spine. "Did I scare you? I was fine. Textbook. I've ridden way ranker bulls on the tour," he said softly keeping his voice low so as to not sound like he was bragging or to offend any of the more local, amateur cowboys. He'd been one himself as a youngster. "What happened, baby?"

Before he'd been so eager to ice his hand, and now all he could think about was holding Lang, comforting her.

"I'm just so happy to see you and that you're okay." Her voice was muffled around his neck. "And I saw all those cowboys fall and Bodhi got hurt."

"Bodhi's fine. He's getting an X-ray. That's the party line anyway, but he'll meet us at the dinner later. I'm going to take care of his horse, and then you and I can get out of here if you want."

She stiffened in his arms, and then struggled a bit. He eased her down.

"Sorry," she said. "I don't know what happened to me. Sorry."

"No need to apologize." She was not meeting his gaze. She was not okay. Or fine. Or anywhere in between.

"I got your shirt wet."

"What's really going on?"

She looked up at him, her beautiful whiskey-colored gaze troubled and embarrassed. Her eyes cut toward his granddad and Beck and Ashni, who were chatting and doing their best to not look their way.

A wave of love rolled over him. God, he loved his family. He loved his town.

"You can help me get the horses settled. I need to also store my gear and rigging." He put his arm around her and pulled her tight to his body. "Wouldn't mind a shower after, maybe at your place." He kept talking so she could pull herself together. Her head rested between his shoulder and his chest, and he couldn't remember when anything had ever felt so right.

He caught Beck's WTF look, and infinitesimally shrugged.

"We'll see to the horses and catch up with you later at the dinner." Bowen put more power in his voice so that Lang would have some privacy to tell him what was really bothering her. If Mason had hung around to cause her any problems, he might be sporting a bruise on a different side of his face and from his fist this time.

"Okay, we're alone now," he soothed as they walked back toward the livestock area.

They weren't really. There were a lot of people around—

volunteers and staff and cowboys who'd crapped out so instead they packed up and headed out.

She swallowed hard a couple of times and looked to still be struggling with control.

"Did Mason…?"

"No." She shook her head. "No. God no. That seems so long ago."

"It was yesterday."

She huffed out a breath, ran her fingers through her tight, soft curls and then, still not looking at him, she grabbed a currycomb and began to brush Raider, Beck's horse.

Being with horses always soothed him so he left her alone and went to get a few more wheelbarrows of sawdust for bedding for the night.

He dumped a load outside Raider's stall and went back for a second load for his horse and Bodhi's.

Langston spread out the bedding, her movements graceful and efficient. No one would know that it had been years since she had considered a barn a second home.

She retrieved a hose and filled up the water.

"My father's here," she whispered.

"Here?" Of all the things she could have said, her dad hadn't even been on his radar. "You saw him?"

"He spoke to me."

Bowen put the hoof pick down. He approached Langston with as much caution as he would a new, untrained horse.

"What did he want?"

"That's what I asked." She crossed her arms and leaned back against Raider, who shuffled a little but surprisingly let her use him as a crutch. "He looks good. Really good. Thin but healthy. I..."

"Was not expecting that," he said slowly trying to remember the last time he'd seen him. He'd been sixteen maybe? Seventeen? Her dad had been a bit of a mentor that summer when Bowen had finally confessed his dream to his granddad that he wanted to pursue the rodeo as a career. His granddad had been game but had suggested he finish college first and compete on the collegiate rodeo teams before making any final decisions. His granddad had been all about keeping all doors open.

And the only door he'd wanted to walk through had been the rodeo for a few years and then to settle down on the ranch with his cousins. Build an honest life they could be proud of.

"He wanted me to know he's sober. That he hasn't gambled in over eight years." Her voice was hard.

"That's good news," he said, feeling his way.

Langston kicked at the ground a little.

"For him." She scrunched up her face. "I hate that he's here. I hate that he's come back. It feels so manipulative."

Bowen didn't answer. "Does he want forgiveness?"

Bowen could imagine he might. He didn't think he could live with himself if he did his woman and his child wrong like that. He didn't think even a one-hundred-step class would be enough to forgive himself. But that wasn't what she needed to hear.

"He said he knew he didn't deserve it, but that he was going to try to build a relationship with me, but that he knew it would take work."

Bowen was at a loss. Forging a relationship with her father would be a good thing—if he was sincere. If he was truly sober and building a productive healthy life. But what did Lang want? He knew she needed her family, but if they couldn't love and support her consistently, he didn't want the man anywhere near Lang.

Not my call.

But the strength of his reaction floored him. Again a rush of gratitude hit him for his granddad and cousins. And even, he thought grudgingly, his mom. She hadn't approved of his rodeo dreams or his love of Montana, but she hadn't stood in his way. She'd always let him spend the bulk of his holidays with his granddad. He'd always thought maybe that was because she hadn't wanted him around. But maybe she'd known he needed the male influence.

"Did he say anything else?"

"He had plenty to say." She grabbed some feed for all three of the horses. Raider and Cash snuffled at her, and a smile flitted across her face before it was gone. She scratched Raider's ears.

"He bought some land and built a house somewhere near Copper Mountain. Only ranch I know of up there is the Wyatt property, and I'm sure they're still up there ranching.

So not sure where my bio dad is, and I don't care."

"You have time," he said, taking her into his arms. "This was his first approach."

"I'm not taking the next step," she said. Still she was pliant in his arms and he walked her back toward the gate so he could kiss her properly.

"You don't have to decide anything now," Bowen said, his lips brushing against hers.

"How would you feel if your dad showed up and wanted to suddenly pretend that the past could be swept away?" She chased his mouth with hers.

"Shocked as hell," he admitted, breathing her in. "But I would hope that I would hear him out." He deepened the kiss, and she wrapped her arms around him, and her fingers played with his hair. "Eventually."

She laughed against his mouth. "I think we both lack interpersonal skills," she murmured.

"Our skills are just fine." He pulled back a little. "Family's family."

"You have a family," she snarked.

"You do too, Lang. Maybe just give it some time, hey?"

She scowled but then cuddled against him. He found himself smiling.

"I like taking care of the horses with you, Dandelion." He ruffled her hair wanting to lighten the mood and also to get his hard-on to settle down.

"Another euphemism." She smiled. "So let's take care of these boys and then I'll take care of you."

And just like that his desire flared.

"I like that you watched me ride today," he murmured. "I haven't had that before."

"You like to be watched," she teased him and nipped his bottom lip.

He laughed, feeling happiness pour into him like a shot of top-shelf whiskey. "You've got plenty of admirers watching you, Bowen Ballantyne."

"No one like you. Not a one."

THAT NIGHT AS the sky faded to purple, and the lights in the trees of the park turned on, Langston sipped from her iced tea and watched Bowen and Bodhi talk bulls with several Wilder men—locals who had been bull riders and now bred top-tier bulls and provided stock for the American Extreme Bull Riding Tour, and the western rodeos on the pro rodeo tour. They also worked with another ranch to provide bulls for local rodeos in several western states.

She hadn't imagined that she'd have had an appetite after the encounter with her father this afternoon, but after her humiliating and unexpected sob fest that Bowen had absorbed with enviable calm, she was hungry. That might have been due to the intense bout of against-the-wall sex at her apartment because neither of them had been able to wait as she'd fumbled with her key.

She didn't realize she was staring at Bowen until Ben Ballantyne nudged her.

"He's a good man."

She blinked and felt herself flush. She'd been so busted, but what could she say? It was absolutely true.

"I knew that when I was eleven," she said.

I wish he were mine.

She swallowed the wish. She was supposed to act crazy in love. Not like she was dreading saying goodbye.

The problem was, she'd fallen into the trap of her own design.

"It's good you're back home where you belong," Ben Ballantyne said, looking pleased.

She didn't want to lie to him. He was such a good, solid man. He deserved his ranch and his family around him, growing, thriving as he aged, not a game.

"My job at the Graff is only for the year," she said, sneaking a quick look at Bowen.

"Sure you'll find something else before then," he said lightly touching her hand. "A year is a long time."

She'd figured it was long enough for her to plan for the next stage of her life.

But she hadn't counted on her father barging back into her life. And she definitely hadn't imagined having to get over Bowen.

The wave crashed over her then. She loved him. She always had. And it was going to take everything she had to walk away with a smile, like she'd told him she could during their picnic. Unlike her father and Mason, Langston kept her promises.

Feeling helpless she glanced at Bowen again. Thank God he was not looking at her. Good thing bulls were so fascinating.

"I heard you had a visitor today."

If one could call being snuck up on at a rodeo standing amidst thousands of people a visitor, then yeah.

"Did Bowen tell you?"

"No. I've been in touch on and off with your dad over the years."

Of course he had. Ben knew everyone and had a big heart. And she supposed hers was hard and shriveled.

"You don't know the whole story, Langston."

"I don't want to know it," she said quickly.

"Fair enough."

"Bowen thinks I should give myself time before deciding if I want to talk to him again."

"Time can't hurt, but only you should make the decision. Not me. Not Bowen."

Always alone.

"He wanted to talk to you earlier—when you were in Helena and engaged—but he thought that would make trouble for you because of Mason's family and his past."

Langston winced, somehow feeling her father probably thought she'd reached for higher stars than she'd been entitled to and had been justly knocked back down. And maybe she had, but she'd fallen for Mason because he'd represented family and connections to her—safety.

She'd wanted to belong.

Was she doing the same thing with the Ballantynes? They had always represented family and connection and belonging that she'd craved. But Bowen...Bowen had been special to her since the beginning.

"I told your dad you were back in town working local and no longer engaged to some stuffed shirt, entitled political wannabe. I told him you and Bowen had finally found each other."

Finally?

She stared at Ben, confused by that statement.

"Why'd you tell him anything?" She wanted to be angry, but Ben was so...so...Ben. Kind. Steady. No pushover. He was smart. Honest. And he had a playful side that people didn't see coming until it hit them—like a sneaker wave. He obviously harbored no grudge toward her biological father.

But she was so tired of being hurt. Abandoned.

And Bowen would leave the end of next week.

And yet, if she kept holding on to her hurt, she'd be unable to reach for something good. Wasn't that what this year was supposed to be all about?

"I didn't want you to run into him without warning. I wanted to give you some time to think. I wanted him to feel welcomed back in Marietta."

Which meant he'd invited her dad to the Ballantyne Bash. But she didn't want him welcomed back even though she knew that was unfair. Trust Ben to smooth the way home for her, for her father.

Langston pushed her plate away, no longer hungry. She'd enjoyed the conversation with Bowen's family far more than the food. She still had tonight and tomorrow with Bowen. Maybe even a few days next week. She needed to enjoy the time she had, not mourn for the time she wouldn't get. And maybe if she kept reminding herself of that, she'd finally believe it.

"Ready for some dessert?" Bowen turned toward her, and his face was unexpectedly close. Her heart clenched. He was so, so handsome. She could stare at him forever.

"Definitely."

"I meant the G-rated kind that jacks up our blood sugar."

"Me too," she demurred but let her eyes showed her wicked intent.

"Behave," he murmured in her ear. "And help me get some crumble for the table."

They'd just made it back with handfuls of dessert when a beautiful young woman with a slightly punk look and exaggerated makeup bounced up.

"Bowen, I need, need, need a solid," she said.

"Sure, what's up, Dylan?"

Langston blinked. This was Dylan? Dylan Telford? She remembered her as being a couple of years younger than her at school. She had always been dreamy and artistic, and a little bit wild. She'd known that Dylan had headed out to LA to break into the rock music scene. She'd been having success. Climbing the charts and getting a lot of notice on social media, but then the band had imploded.

Langston was a bit shocked she'd come home to Marietta. There didn't seem to be many opportunities for musicians who'd already had a taste of fame.

"The opening band canceled, and the Prairie Dogs won't start early. I was going to jump in and play a few covers and then a few of my originals, but I think folks will think I'm showing off if it's just me. Please, please, please play a few songs with me."

"Dylan." Bowen stared at her, his hands full of plates of crumble. "I'm self-taught and I just noodle on my own to pass time. I've done some open mics here and there—nothing like this." He jerked his head toward the crowd.

"Bowen, the crowd has nothing to do with it. You perform in front of thousands every weekend. I know you write songs, and Bodhi outed that you still play. And I know you write some songs, BB Tyne." She grinned at him, and Langston felt like she was outside looking in.

Dylan looked beseechingly at her. "Don't let this cowboy leave me hanging. Langston. Help me out."

Langston tried to stem the rush of pleasure—she really did—when Dylan assumed that she might have some sway over Bowen.

"You have a great voice," Langston said. "You used to entertain us during the summer rodeos when we were kids, and participate in the talent section of the fair. You said you'd done some songwriting. Don't hold out on your hometown."

Dylan looked thrilled. Langston was dubious Bowen could go up and sing with a rock star—former rock star.

"Figures Bodhi would rat me out."

"It's a challenge," Langston goaded. "I thought you Ballantynes thrived on challenges."

"Certain challenges." Bowen looked at his granddad. "Did you put Bodhi up to this?"

"You can't do a neighbor a favor?" Ben asked. "I raised you better than that. You drag that guitar around with you everywhere. You hide your talents away. Take a chance," Ben said. "I dare you."

There it was. The Ballantyne slap-down challenge. "Now it's family, pride on the line," Langston said. "I dare you," she mouthed.

Bowen stood. "Challenge accepted."

BOWEN QUICKLY TUNED his guitar. "What did you have in mind?" he asked Dylan. He couldn't believe he was doing this—performing publicly in Marietta without even one rehearsal. There was no way he would have considered it, except for his granddad's dare, and how Langston also flew that flag. She hadn't missed a beat. He loved her spirit.

Loved?

He was in trouble with her. He was in way too deep.

And now, as he plugged a borrowed chord into Dylan's amp and they ran a quick sound check, he found himself buzzing with excitement—much like he did before he hopped on the back of a bull.

Langston stood close to the edge of the stage, gazing up at him, and he'd be lying if he didn't say that's what gave him such a buzz—the stars in her eyes, her smile, the way she looked at him like he'd done something special.

She deserved a man who could give her the world. She'd been let down so many times by so many men. And he was going to be one more.

How could he be so careless with her heart?

She'd agreed. It was a game. Fun. A way to help Granddad, but Bowen had a feeling they were both in too deep, and it was all going to go spectacularly sideways.

"Hey," Dylan suggested. "Let's start with something slow and moody."

Sounded right to him. He looked at Langston, and in her beautiful amber eyes he could see forever.

I don't have to leave.

The though came out of nowhere. But in truth it hadn't. The first time he'd kissed her, he'd felt a rightness. A sense of being home, belonging. Walking with her and chatting over several hours his first night home had formed a connection he'd never had with a woman.

And then he'd blown it by playing her game and drawing her into his.

"Do you know Taylor Swift's 'Exile'? You'd kill on the Bon Iver part."

Bowen couldn't think of a more appropriate song to kick

off his night of the too-late epiphany.

And as he fingerpicked his way through the song, accompanying Dylan, who played a keyboard, he never once shifted his gaze off of Langston. He wanted her to know that even if this all blew up in their faces like he knew it would, she meant something to him.

Everything.

LANGSTON RECORDED THE performance. She wanted to have it to remember this night—the night where she'd come back fully into her life. She was home in Marietta, and even if she left in a year, she would have closure on her past. Even if she didn't agree to see her father again, he had reached out to her. He had realized his mistakes and had made a supreme effort to rebuild his life. If she couldn't find it in herself to forgive him, at least she could be happy that he was healthy and had rebuilt his life and found some peace.

She still didn't like the idea of giving him a chance. She still felt so raw, but maybe if she shut him out, it would hurt her as much as him. How could she open her heart and trust a man if she still clung to her past childhood of being hurt, disappointed and abandoned? People said that you repeated patterns in your life. Had she picked Mason because subconsciously she'd recognized that he was incapable of truly bonding with her?

What did that say about her future if she chose the same

sort of man over and over? She would be doomed. She'd never have the family she craved.

Bowen's not like that.

She shut down her inner voice of hope. Of course Bowen was different. He also wasn't hers. What they had going on wouldn't last.

She was so proud of Bowen. He seemed so comfortable on the stage. He sang a few country hits, and he and Dylan sang several duets. From agreeing to sing several songs, he'd ended up singing far more, and when he finally unplugged and slung his guitar around to his back, leaving Dylan to sing a few of her songs, Lang wanted to run off with him.

But that wouldn't be fair. He had so many friends and family here who would want to congratulate him—for his high score today and now the impromptu concert.

He stepped into her arms, and she slid her arms around his waist, anchoring them under his guitar.

"I want to dance with you, and I want to get out of here and be alone with you in equal measure."

"Equal?"

"That was me trying to be polite. I'd mostly like to make a run for it, but I promised you a dance or two."

"You did, Bowen Ballantyne." She stood on tiptoes. "We can dance at my place." She nipped his ear. "Naked."

"Definitely on the agenda," he murmured in her ear. "But first I want to hold you and dance under the lights and the stars like I promised."

They danced several dances, and then when former LA

rocker Eddie Cole got up on stage with Dylan to thunderous applause, Bowen found himself once again called up to play. He joined them on another two songs with Eddie taking lead vocals—his shaggy blond hair, leather and tattoos fitting in far more during a guitar solo than they did as he walked around downtown Marietta where he'd recently opened a music store.

Dylan and Eddie called it a night as the Prairie Dogs—the headliner for the night—waited in the wings. Bowen jumped down. Took her hand like he'd been doing it for years, and he and Langston walked back to his truck to make the short drive back to her apartment.

There was so much she wanted to say, but all of it felt too heavy and too honest for what they had promised each other. Bowen didn't seem to feel a need to chat either.

It felt so right for him to close the door behind them. Lock it and then slowly undress her, his eyes holding hers while she undressed him, and this time instead of the urgent passion that had always made Langston keen on the edge of losing her sense of self, he took her to bed and made love to her slowly, lingering, exploring her body as if they had all night, and when he finally entered her slick heat, she tangled her fingers in his hair and clamped her jaw shut so she wouldn't utter the fatal words that had drummed in her brain all week.

Chapter Thirteen

Bowen had rosined his rope earlier in the day, but he couldn't stop running it through his gloved hand. He wasn't nervous. He felt good about the bull he'd pulled. He was in first place going into the finals. He'd stretched and was healthy. His hold hand hurt less today than he'd expected after his ride yesterday. It was something else that kept niggling at the back of his brain. Wouldn't let go.

Langston. Last night, seeing how she stared up at him while he was on stage, singing along with the songs she knew, it had hit him square in his chest: this was not a hookup. Langston had never been a hookup. He'd tried to do the right thing and keep it all in the court of a game, but they'd crossed out of bounds days ago. Or at least he had.

So where did that leave him?

Did he tell her he wanted to make them real?

Ask her to give him a chance? Wait for him? Lots of couples had to do long-distance on occasion.

But were they a couple? Bowen had never thought about himself in those terms, but he was liking the idea more than a lot.

But did she feel the same, his Dandelion?

He made a rude sound and pushed off the wall. A few cowboys who were also trying to find their Zen, or whatever anyone chose to call it, looked irritated as he stomped past.

He had to get out of his head. Had to examine his feelings later or never.

He had a job to do first.

Then he could talk to Lang and see how things went. Her here. Him on the road. Maybe he should wait to see what was going on with Granddad.

Coward.

No commitment.

Like every other man in her life.

Still, he resolved to talk to her after the rodeo. She could take it from there.

Feeling more settled he walked toward the chutes, Beck and Bodhi flanking him. It felt good to have his cousins there. Bodhi wore his usual mile-wide smile even though he had to be in pain from the hairline fracture from yesterday.

"You could—" Beck started to say.

"Nah," Bodhi interrupted.

"This rodeo doesn't count for your rankings," Beck doggedly continued, not for the first time that day since Bodhi had already competed in saddleless bronc final—which he'd won. "You already got the pride earlier. Let your wrist rest another week."

"I got two more competitions today. Not scratching on either. Are you?"

"Nah." Beck smiled—a secret, smirky smile Bowen recognized from too many times in their youth when Beck thought he was going to pull one over on both of them. "I'm all in."

"Me too." Bodhi patted the pocket of his protective vest—startling Bowen.

"Wait, what? You bought Nico a ring?" His voice rang out. "Not for reals. Let me see."

"Not something you show your cousin before your girl, a lesson you may want to heed. Or not," Bodhi taunted.

Both Beck and Bodhi turned their attention toward him, and it took Bowen most of his self-control to not squirm. They were taking the game too far.

But you are going to ask Lang to make us real.

"Focus on your ride, Romeo. You don't want to dim that smile of yours by eating a mouthful of dirt."

Bodhi's ride was exquisite. He hung on like nothing was wrong, like he was riding for prize and glory and just for the sheer excitement of living.

But Bowen's ride scored two points better. He loved the fact that his family was here—all of them, his mom and aunts and Langston. She was sitting with Granddad and a few of his friends. All day he'd felt an invisible thread connecting them.

He stood in the winner's circle, getting asked the couple of obligatory questions. Then his buckle and check. A few pictures for the paper. A short interview after. He savored the moment as he got to pose with his granddad who'd made his way down and a few other members from the rodeo committee including Taryn Telford, whose son Ronan he'd competed with in the summer teen rodeo circuit.

He smiled and waved to the crowd, his eyes unerringly going to where Langston sat in the family section.

And that scared the hell out of him.

LANGSTON CUT OUT after the finals, texting Bowen that she'd meet him at the ranch as she was helping prepare a few things for the Bash. A lie. She was running. It had been between spreading a homemade mustard on a still-steaming pretzel and pulling off a piece that Langston had realized she couldn't do this anymore. Pretend. Lie. Game play.

Sitting in the stands with the Ballantyne family and the Telfords and the Wilders had been every dream she'd ever had as a kid. Family and friends coming together to celebrate and cheer on loved ones. Only this time she was a part of it—included.

Except she wasn't. Not really. Sure, she and Bowen were having a fling, but it was a favor. They weren't really dating. He wasn't really falling in love with her. Whereas she had fallen deep, fast.

She should have seen this disaster galloping toward her. Bowen was everything she ever dreamed of in a man, but so much more, and she was still her. Langston Carr. Girl left behind.

She'd held the pretzel and stared at the rodeo queen's

glitz and glam, beautiful racing across the arena, flags held proudly, but suddenly the rodeo and afternoon had seemed as pointless as her heart. She had known this would happen. She'd just thought she could handle it better when Bowen pulled out of town and they "drifted" apart.

She promised herself she'd be fine, but she knew that was a lie, and even the desperate prayer to enjoy the moment and make some memories fell flat, no matter how many times she reminded herself.

Ben Ballantyne had shared her pretzel and asked what she was thinking about—he'd worried that she was still upset about running into her father after so many years, but truthfully, even though she still didn't know if she'd be ready to give her father another chance after so long, she was far more concerned with Bowen taking off on tour.

Ben's kind eyes had sucked out an honest, raw reply. "It hit me that it's all going to be over in a few days," she'd confessed. "Bowen will head back out on the road."

"Life of a cowboy." Ben's reply had been blunt, but his expression sympathetic.

"Yes." She'd swallowed. "I know."

Did she ever.

The realization that she was on borrowed time now played in her mind over and over as Langston neared the turn-off for Three Tree Ranch. She blinked furiously, determined not to cry even as the tears spilled over and tracked down her face. She hit the steering wheel. No. No tears. She'd known what she was getting into.

She paused at the turn, tempted to just keep driving—out of town, out of state, just out and away as if she could out-drive the awful, hot, heavy feeling that crushed her chest.

This was her fault. She'd known her heart would jump in where it wasn't wanted and get crushed in the process. Watching Bowen ride today, and win, hit home how much he was a true cowboy. He loved the competition, pitting his skills against the animals and other competitors. As she'd watched him receive his buckle and prize money, her last thread of hope severed. He loved the rodeo and he needed to be free to live out his dream.

She'd been toying with the idea of seeing if he wanted to keep it casual and see each other when he was back in town. That would give them the tour break, the holidays and a few stolen moments in between. But after seeing him ride and decisively win over Bodhi, she realized that would never work. He'd have pressure that he didn't need, and she had to be honest. She'd lose in that tug-of-war. He already felt responsible for so many. She didn't want to add to his burden.

She hadn't been enough for her father to stay. What made her think she could hold a man like Bowen?

She'd come to Marietta determined to take the year and rebuild her life. She needed to focus on that. And maybe try to build something with her father. They couldn't repair the past, but maybe she could create a future that wasn't so broken so that someday she would find a man she could trust to stay.

BOWEN RUSHED THROUGH packing up. Beck and Ashni had already headed off to the ranch. He and Bodhi had shared a rig since they'd only brought one horse each for the roping demonstrations and competition, but Bowen had sent Bodhi off with Nico, telling him that he'd trailer the horses and get them settled back at the ranch.

He'd wanted the time alone with Langston. To talk with her. Feel her out. Come to some sort of understanding. This was a mess. He didn't want to pretend anymore because Langston felt more real than anything he'd had with any other woman. But it wasn't fair to her to keep up the pretense.

He wanted honesty between them, even though they'd started with a pretense.

Bowen tried to shake off his dark thoughts. Her text saying that she was heading early to the ranch to help with some last-minute details shouldn't make him so edgy. The moms had pulled out all the stops. But still it felt like a dodge. Bowen had no idea what tonight would bring—would Beck propose? Was Bodhi playing with Nico, or had he finally found a woman who could hold him? How far was he prepared to take it? And would their granddad reconsider?

Bowen wouldn't have any answers until he found Langston and could ask the one question, the only question that mattered to him—was she willing to take a chance with him?

Was what they had real? Worth pursuing?

Getting out of the rodeo grounds was easier said than done. The local paper, the *Courier* caught up with him and he granted a short interview. Lots of local cowboys wanted to talk. And then there were the kids and their families, and Bowen forced himself to be patient, kind as so many cowboys had been to him when he'd been a kid.

But he'd be lying if he said his nerves weren't consuming him by the time he'd returned to the ranch, stabled the horses, checked on their water and feed and then took a quick shower before heading up to Plum Hill.

The party wasn't yet in full swing. A local country band played. Groups sat around, laughing, talking, drinking. The bonfires had yet to be lit. Several food trucks were parked off to the side of the festivities. The barn was lit up like Christmas. And all Bowen could do was scan the crowd looking for Lang. And then he spotted her, walking quickly out of the cabin, her heart-shaped face tight. She twisted her fingers together, her eyes searched his, looking for what he didn't know.

The burbling tension he'd tried to shut down since he'd received her text now choked him as he walked up the hill from the parking area to greet her.

"What's up?" he asked wanting to pull her into his arms and promise her that everything would be okay, but he couldn't make that promise. Hell, nothing felt okay at the moment. Even the high over his win had faded.

"I'm sorry, Bowen," Lang said, her voice taut as a guitar

string. "I know I promised to see this through, but I can't. I can't. I need to break up with you."

Langston's eyes were huge and swimmy with tears. "I know we're not real and I'm letting you down, but I can't pretend. I can't do it anymore."

He heard her words even over all the noise of the party. But none of them made any sense. The past few days had been the best and happiest in his life. He wanted more with her.

And now she was breaking up with him?

"Ummmm. Okay." What else could he say?

"I'm not good at deception like Mason and my cousin and my dad. And I don't want to be. The past few days working at the house with your mom and aunts and the steak dinner and sitting with your granddad in the stands today was everything I ever wanted." Her words tumbled over each other. "It felt so real. Being with you felt real. I know it was fake and a game, and we were just playing, but I don't think I ever was. I think when I fell in love with you at sixteen, which I know sounds ridiculous, that was it. That was real. And everyone else was just a poor substitute. The opposite to make me forget, only I didn't forget. I couldn't and then this week..." She was openly crying.

"I fell so hard, Bowen. Really hard." Her beautiful whiskey-colored eyes glimmered in the twilight. "But I can't do this. I can't pretend to not feel something when I feel so much. I can't deceive good people. And I can't accept a one-sided relationship or a relationship where I'm the only one invested. Not again."

"I didn't want to hurt you," he began, screaming at himself to think. To speak. To say the magic words that would make this right, but he'd never been good with words, with explanations. That was Bodhi. Not him.

"I know," she said and brushed along his cheekbone with her knuckles. He turned his face in to kiss her hand, but she pulled back. "You are the kindest man. A good man. This is not your fault. We started out wrong, but I should have known better. I was already in before I even knew what was happening. I've always had it bad for you, Bowen." Her voice broke off in a half laugh, half sob. "It was a bit of a joke between my granddad and yours so many years ago, as if my feelings as a teenager were amusing.

"But what I felt then was not a joke. It was real. And what I feel now is..." She sighed, and it seemed as if all of her sparkle dimmed, leaving her deflated. "And that's why I have to break up even though we were never real. I can't pretend and I can't be casual and happily wave goodbye next weekend and act like nothing happened."

He stood there like a block of wood facing the bonfire. *Say something.* Anything, but his mind just uselessly spun, words floating by, none of them in a context that would prove useful. She was leaving him.

"Even if you do have some...feelings for me..." she gulped in a deep breath and squared her shoulders just like he'd seen her do a million times as a kid before she mounted Buttercup to head into the arena to compete, to win "...they aren't enough. I can't hope. I can't wait around. I can't harbor so much inside." She hit her chest a few times. "And be alone hoping that you'll come back to me. Waiting and hoping that you'll come home, just like I waited for my mom and then my dad to come back so many times. Over and over."

He nodded. He was a cowboy. A bull rider like her daddy had been. Most of his life was lived on the road.

"And you deserve to be happy, Bowen. I saw that today with your ride. You are so gifted. You need to live your best life and follow your dream. Not feel guilt when you're away or feel like you have to atone when you are home." She closed her eyes, briefly and then opened them, and they shone with a fierce light. "Goodbye, Bowen."

And then she was gone, walking quickly down the hill toward her car. He couldn't watch her go. He turned around and saw the glow of the lights, the chords of the music, the dim, lilting voices of the gathering crowd. He was home. And this time, for the first time, he felt completely alone, like he didn't belong.

He hadn't wanted to play the Rodeo Bride Game, but yet he had. He'd gone balls to the wall as Bodhi would say, and yet just like Langston, his heart had been all in before he'd even decided to play.

But she was right. She couldn't be the woman left at home waiting for her man to return. Ash had chosen to follow Beck. She'd made a life for them on the road, but he couldn't ask that of Langston. She needed a home. A family.

A man who stayed.

He walked up the hill toward the light and laughter, never feeling quite so in the dark and cut adrift.

"Took you long enough." His granddad broke off from a group of friends. "Come help me get the bonfires going."

He followed, feeling like he was having an out-of-body experience—having to think about coordinating his limbs. The wood had been stacked. He and Beck and Bodhi had made a bit of a Jenga game out of it Friday morning.

This morning the crew had added more kindling and some paper scraps in some of the spaces to help with airflow.

"You're not really leaving the ranch, are you?" he asked his granddad.

His granddad didn't falter as he walked around the first fire pit, checking the structure for safety.

"Three Tree Ranch is your heart and soul."

His granddad looked at him across from the stacked wood. "My family's my heart and soul. My girls. You, Bodhi and Beck and his Ashni. I've always been about family."

"Me too," he said.

"I know." His granddad smiled, and it had a mischievous tilt to it. "But sometimes you have to be selfish."

Bowen stared at him, not understanding. He'd always been the eldest. It was his job to watch out for the others. He didn't have the luxury to think about what he wanted. If he did, he'd be chasing Langston, begging her for a chance to prove that he could be the man she wanted and needed. That he could be the man who would stay. He wanted to be that man so badly he was choking on it.

"Sometimes you have to cut ties," his granddad said, handing him a second fire stick.

Or someone else did it for you.

"I disagree."

"How so?"

He stared at his granddad across the wide circle—the stack of wood in the shape of a tall Christmas tree between them.

"I can't cut ties. The ranch. The town. The people. The community. The traditions. My family. All of it is me. This place, the land, the life. It's in my DNA. Without it I don't know who'd I'd be."

His granddad watched him for a beat. Two. Three. What did he see? His granddad's opinion had always been the most vital to him.

"I don't want you to hurt her."

"She's the one who walked." He didn't even try to hide it from his granddad. He always knew their hearts. He knew when they were up to mischief before they'd even hatched the plan. He'd always known them.

"If Lang is your choice for no other reason—" his granddad leveled his best "man up" stare "—then she is the woman you want to build a life with wherever that is. I suggest you run after her, son. Give her a reason to stay."

His granddad bent down and lit the one section of the bonfire.

Bowen stood there, fists clenched. Heart pounding like

he'd run a race. "She walked," he repeated. "She left me. She needs more than me."

"That girl has always known what she wants," his granddad said, the flames starting to lick up the kindling. He gestured roughly down the hill. "I didn't raise quitters."

"You knew," he accused, raw with sudden insight.

"You boys think you're so clever. I sat next to Lang today trying to get a read on her feelings for you, how genuine they were, and they run soul deep. She couldn't take her eyes off you when you rode, and that's when I knew she was in love, and it's the kind of love that sticks. And that's the love you deserve. But you never listen to your heart. You do what you think you should, what others expect, not necessarily what you want to do. I think she knows that, and she knows she can't build a life with you while waiting for you to walk back in the front door. So…" He lit another section of the kindling. The flames whooshed and started to lick up the pyre.

He stood and stared Bowen down. "Heart check. Do you run after your girl, or you going to stand around gutted, wondering what your cousins will or won't do? Decide. Help me light the other bonfires. Or chase down your future." His granddad held out his hand for the fire stick, as if he had no doubt the side Bowen would come down on.

The stick slapped his granddad's outstretched palm and Bowen took off back down the hill at a run.

Chapter Fourteen

"Dang it. Bodhi Ballantyne, you are a jerk of epic proportions," Langston shouted out to no one in particular.

Although people did hear her. A lot of them since carloads of couples, friends and families were arriving, carrying blankets and camp chairs and food or drink to share and heading up the path—lit by solar lights that she and Bowen had installed Friday night.

Bowen. Everything went back to Bowen. And she'd wanted to race out of here in a plume of dust before she lost her will and broke down and accepted whatever crumbs he was willing to drop at her feet. But Bodhi Mister Too Cool barely a mortal had to go and block her in with his dang monster truck. Why? He'd parked parallel to two cars in the section reserved for family and workers like the most arrogant idiot in the world. So she was trapped. And so was someone else. Unless she wanted to commit grand-theft auto. And she could have her own video game going on tonight, as hotwiring a truck was one of the skills her dad had stuck around long enough to teach her.

She actually stomped her foot. "Ballantyne men are the

most arrogant, cock-sure…"

"I hope sexy's in that list at some point," a soft voice interrupted her tirade.

She spun around. Bowen. Her heart took off faster than she'd wanted to race out of here.

"I know stupid is."

"Definitely," she said breathlessly.

He was here. Right here. Close enough to touch. All of her senses tunneled, so that she didn't see more cars driving along the gravel road slowly, hear people parking, calling out to each other, walking past them. The band.

"Madly, crazy in love should top the list."

And she just lost the ability to breathe. And to swallow.

"Bowen…what are you saying?"

"What I should have said when you dumped me ten minutes ago. I'm boots over head, flat on my back, breath knocked out of me in love with you, Dandelion."

"Dandelion," she repeated. "That's how you're going to confess that you love me? Calling me a weed?"

"I love dandelions. I told you that. They are my favorite flower."

She frowned.

"They are resilient. Small but mighty. They bloom a brilliant yellow and then pull a neat trick and turn the color of a summer cloud and dance in the breeze, singing to the wind to carry them away to their next adventure."

"I think you hit your head today." Langston took a step toward him.

"Dandelions endure. They tease with their beauty and carry our hopes and dreams."

She took another step wanting to crush the distance between them. "No one has ever said anything so wonderful to me," she admitted, swiping away a few tears. She'd already touched up her makeup once today after her miserable dash back to the ranch. She didn't want to have to again.

"I always admired your spirit when we were kids. You were so alone, but so fierce and competitive and all mouth when there were so many times I didn't know what to say, you always jumped in."

"Open mouth. Speak. Think. That's me."

He pulled her into his arms, and she nestled into him, feeling like she belonged. "I don't ever want to pretend," she said, "ever again."

"I was never pretending," he admitted. "From the beginning what we had felt real. I just didn't know how to trust it."

"I don't want to deceive Ben."

"I don't think we could if we tried." He kissed the top of her head. "Not that I want to. This is real, Langston." He pulled apart a little to take her hand in his and press it against his heart. You and me. I want us to be real. I want us to be forever."

"Me too, Bowen. Me too."

He kissed her, and Langston felt that the night had become surreal, a dream, and she didn't even want to try to wake up. After who knew how long, he broke the kiss and then laughed.

"Bodhi must have known I'd eff it up with you tonight since he blocked you and someone else in."

"Maybe I shouldn't have been cursing him then." Lang jammed both hands into the back pockets of Bowen's Wranglers. God, he had an amazing butt. And body. But that was only the beginning of the list of things she loved, loved, loved about him.

"You should regularly curse him," Bowen said.

"But you said he came up with the rodeo bride idea. If he hadn't, you probably wouldn't have given me a second glance."

"Bodhi likes to think he's all that, but he's not. I like to think I am not that blind or dumb," Bowen argued, cupping her faced and stroking her cheeks with his thumbs. "We would have still found each other."

Langston had no idea how long they stood by her car gazing at each other; the music and voices a pleasant background blur.

"I don't know what's going to go down tonight," he said, smiling. "But it's sure to be entertaining. Do you want to be my date to the Bash, and I'll be yours?"

"I'd like that," she said standing on her tiptoes to kiss him. "For many, many years to come."

"I can't promise that," he said, taking her hand in his and playing with her fingers. "I don't know if we'll have the ranch, but we'll have each other, and we'll figure the rest out."

"You're all I'll ever need, Bowen Ballantyne."

"I'll do for a start," he said. "But there's a lot more to come, and that's a promise I can make and keep."

They walked up the path, following other guests. Langston, holding on to Bowen's hand, felt like she had wings.

He snagged them two beers and stood in the short line for a grilled cheese sandwich at the Melt food truck.

"Hey, Bowen, I heard you sing last night with Dylan," the owner Raelynn Woods said cheerfully as she took their order. "And then of course Eddie had to jump on stage. You and Eddie and Dylan should form a trio. Take over Flint-Works on a regular schedule. You all sounded so good together. His music store is open now: Mistletoe Music. It has a studio and rehearsal space."

"I just might do that, Rae. I'll be around a lot more after the finals so who knows, I might have the time."

They stepped out of the line to wait for their order. Langston debated whether to ask him what that meant or keep her mouth shut and just enjoy the evening.

"Ask me. I can tell you want to."

"When we're alone."

"Alone alone or alone on a hay bale where I'm just thinking about what I want to do to you when we are alone, but not actually doing it?"

"That sounds like a trick question."

Bowen laughed. Her heart soared when just minutes ago she'd thought it had died.

It was amazing, Langston thought in a daze as Rae handed them their two sandwiches and they made their way to sit on a hay bale that was not too close to the fires or the band, but not so far that it would get too chilly.

Bowen shrugged out of his jacket. She'd been too upset to remember where she'd left hers. Somewhere in the cabin, probably when she'd been reading Beck the riot act because he hadn't clued Ashni in on the Rodeo Bride Game.

"I don't want you to quit the rodeo for me, Bowen. I mean it. You love it. You're in your prime. What I said today rings true for me, but it's from my childhood, and fears and feelings can be overcome if I try to discuss them with you."

"Yes," he said, straddling the hay bale so that he could sit close to her. "That's true. Communication is key, but so is discussion. We should talk about things and then make our decision together."

"Yes, but…yum," she murmured as he broke off a piece of his sandwich—smoked Gouda and fresh tomato and pickle—and fed it to her.

"The truth is, I've been going through the motions the past couple of years."

"You have?"

"Habit. And I know I told you I was worried about Bodhi. Beck's seemed lost, drifting. We've all lost our fire, and I think the only thing keeping us going is that no one is willing to step away first."

"Do you want to be the one to step away first?"

"I thought we'd quit together. Come back and work the ranch. We'd need other sources of income. We've all saved, but ranching has lean years. I've sold some songs, and thought I could pursue that. And maybe add horse breeding and training back to the ranch portfolio."

She sat up. "Horses. Really?" Her excitement felt like she'd vibrate off the hay bale.

"Really. Eat while it's hot or I'm going to start gnawing on your share. I'm hungry and since I've got to be polite for quite a bit longer tonight and not eat what I really crave, I'm going to need a different type of fuel to sustain me." He leaned forward and kissed her, and his meaning was very clear. It thrilled her that he wanted her so much. She felt the same, and she wanted to be alone with the same intensity that she craved being here at the party with him. She had a sense of belonging that she'd rarely felt. "So what do you think about horses?" Bowen asked. "I'm going to need a partner to help me breed and train."

"I feel like I've just drunk a bottle of champagne, and it's all fuzzing round inside of me," she confessed. "Horses." She put the sandwich down, too full of joy to eat. "Mason gave me my earnest money back on the townhouse. I didn't think he would. He's a lawyer and he has a lot of connections, so I thought if I fought him it would take more money and time than it was worth."

"You should have told me you were having trouble."

"Well, now I'm not."

"We've got some time to think about it. Obviously what Granddad decides will impact our decisions."

"Our," she repeated, loving the sound of that word.

She'd wanted to be part of an us, a we, for so long. "Whatever we do, Bowen, it's going to be an adventure. I'm going to love it because I love you."

"Say it again."

She scooted closer to him. "I love you."

The expression in his eyes nearly melted her.

"I'm going to finish this year out," he said. "It's likely that I'll be in the finals so it's a couple months more, and then I'm going to tell management that I'm done. I won't be back in January."

"Maybe you should wait before making such a big decision."

"No, I've waited long enough. It's time I thought of myself and what I want, and I don't want to be away from you for months at a time."

It was like hoping for a drop of water or a summer shower and getting an endless waterfall of hope and happiness.

"I've been saving, and I have investments, but it will be a big drop in income because I'll lose all my sponsors," Bowen added.

As if she'd ever care about that. "We'll make it work. I'm signed on to the Graff for the year, and I don't want to back out of that."

"I like that about you, that you don't back out of your promises and commitments."

She switched positions so that she was sitting in the cradle of his legs, her face against his chest and his arms around her. She looked out on the crowd.

"Did you talk to your granddad? Ask him if he really wants to sell the ranch? Tell him about the game?"

She heard Bowen's rumble of laughter. "Not really. He's still playing coy. Mostly we talked about my feelings for you. I'll pin him down tomorrow. I also want to talk to Bodhi and Beck about me not re-signing with the tour. If Granddad wants to sell, maybe we can carve out a parcel for the three of us to start with and buy that or do a lease to own so that he has money and freedom if that's what he wants."

"I can't imagine him not being here."

"Me neither."

"And the game?"

"I'd like to watch Bodhi and Beck play and make fools of themselves." He tilted her face up to his. "But I don't need to play because I've already won."

The End

Want more? Check out Beck and Ashni's story in *The Cowboy Says I Do*!

Join Tule Publishing's newsletter for more great reads and weekly deals!

If you enjoyed *The Cowboy's Challenge*,
you'll love the next book in the…

Montana Rodeo Brides series

Book 1: *The Cowboy Says I Do*

Book 2: *The Cowboy's Challenge*

Book 3: *Breaking the Cowboy's Rules*
Coming January 2022!

Available now at your favorite online retailer!

More books by Sinclair Jayne

The Texas Wolf Brothers series

Book 1: *A Son for the Texas Cowboy*

Book 2: *A Bride for the Texas Cowboy*

Book 3: *A Baby for the Texas Cowboy*

The Wilder Brothers series

Book 1: *Seducing the Bachelor*

Book 2: *Want Me, Cowboy*

Book 3: *The Christmas Challenge*

Book 4: *Cowboy Takes All*

Available now at your favorite online retailer!

About the Author

Sinclair Sawhney is a former journalist and middle school teacher who holds a BA in Political Science and K-8 teaching certificate from the University of California, Irvine and a MS in Education with an emphasis in teaching writing from the University of Washington. She has worked as Senior Editor with Tule Publishing for over seven years.

Writing as Sinclair Jayne she's published fifteen short contemporary romances with Tule Publishing with another four books being released in 2021. Married for over twenty-four years, she has two children, and when she isn't writing or editing, she and her husband, Deepak, are hosting wine tastings of their pinot noir and pinot noir rose at their vineyard Roshni, which is a Hindi word for light-filled, located in Oregon's Willamette Valley. Shaandaar!

Thank you for reading

The Cowboy's Challenge

If you enjoyed this book, you can find more from all our great authors at TulePublishing.com, or from your favorite online retailer.

Made in the USA
Middletown, DE
19 April 2022